Nicholas E W

TANKER

Also by Nicholas E Watkins

Bank

Dealer

Oligarch

Steel

Hack

About the Author

Nicholas Watkins lives on the Coast with his wife and has four children He is a retired Accountant and has a Degree in Economics. He worked in the City of London for many years.

TANKER

Chapter 1

The Hilux pulled up outside the laboratory and parked. The Moon sat low on the horizon and the first red glow of dawn lit up the dry desert sky. All was still, save for the barking of a dog. Security for this sector of the storage facility was in the hands of the Iraqis. Despite being the only thing moving at that time of the morning, the vehicle had not been challenged and no alarms were sounded as it drove into the inner compound.

On paper, the security around the complex of buildings forming the oil storage facility near Basra was impressive. ISIS had looked at it on many occasions as a potential target, but determined that the security presence was too high and their losses would be unacceptable. The laboratory, situated in its own area away from the main buildings, was, in contrast, perceived as far less of a target by the owners. They had neglected it in their assessment of threat levels, so security here was far less comprehensive.

The occupants of the truck sat waiting tensely in the darkness. They were armed with assault rifles, they would have no hesitation in using them if the need arose. They were committed to the aims of ISIS and would happily die as Martyrs in achieving them.

One of the truck's occupants was no more than a boy of sixteen, but he had the hatred of a thousand years in his heart. His Father and Uncles had all opposed the British occupation. It was part of his being, ingrained from childhood. He had seen how the invaders had gradually been defeated, driven back into their compound and finally isolated into a small, defensive position at the airport. He had helped fire the mortars into their base. He had seen their defeat and knew they were weak. He believed, in the end, ISIS would prevail and the Caliphate would be restored.

His companion was slighter in build but older, in his mid-thirties and with a pock marked face. He had been part of Saddam Hussein's army when the invasion had taken place. When the Coalition forces had overthrown the Dictator, they had disbanded the army. It had left him with a gun and no income. He had no love for Hussein and the then ruling Ba'th party but, he at least had an income and had been able to feed his family. It had not taken long for him to become disillusioned with the so called liberators of his Country and he now saw them as an occupying force.

"He should be here by now," said the older of the two. He looked at his watch. They had been there for nearly an hour. They waited another twenty minutes before the door to the laboratory opened and light spilled out across the compound. They jumped from the cab and, slinging their rifles over their shoulders, ran to the beckoning figure.

"Quiet, follow me," said the man in the lab coat. The technician moved swiftly down the corridors, turning left and right. He used his security pass to open doors and led them further into the building. He stopped and pointed to the radioactive symbol and the warning sign above the door. "My pass will take us no further," he said, leaving them outside the door and returning to his job in another part of the building.

The young boy sneaked a look through the glass panel at the top of the door. "Be careful and keep your head down. What did you see?" said his companion.

"Five of them, they are putting their coats on and getting ready to go home." They knew their shift was due to finish at six a.m. the intruders' information was proving to be correct. Unsupervised, they had developed the habit of knocking off early. They waited quietly until the door opened and the workers began to gather up their belongings. The first worker stepped through the door, bidding goodbye to his colleagues. The boy leapt to his feet and struck him in the face with the butt of his rifle, smashing teeth and breaking bone. The technician staggered backwards into his departing colleagues, his hands clutching his bleeding face. The older of the two pointed his rifle at the group, moving it from side to side. They stepped back, dropping their coats and bags to the floor.

"Put your fucking hands down. This isn't a cowboy movie," he said. "You know what we want, so let's not make this difficult for any of us, OK?"

The workers looked at each other, their team leader, an American, decided to speak, "How do you intend to transport it?"

"Just stick it in a box or bag."

"You will be exposed to a massive dose of radiation. More than an hour or two and you will get very ill and possibly die. Do you realise that? This material needs to be handled with extreme caution."

"Do we look like the kind of people who give a fuck? Now stop pissing about and bag it up for us, unless you'd like to die before it kills us." The head technician began the process of removing the radioactive rods from the calibrating machines and placing them in boxes. He and another technician then unlocked the radiation proof safe and removed the rest of the material, stored for intended future use and put it in the bag along with the rods.

"Give us your cell phones." The workers did as they were told, while the duo ripped the internal phones from the walls. "Now, we are trying to let you live, but we need to escape without you causing us a problem. We'll lock you in and smash the key pad on the other side. We know that will only keep you in here for a very short while, but think on this. If you raise the alarm, all of you will be dead by this time tomorrow and all your families will be dead by the time you get home. You are all Iraqis, apart from this man and you live here. We know you. We know your families. We know where you live and we will kill anyone who betrays us." He drew a small pistol and shot the American head of department in the face to underline the message. The rest of the group cowered and watched in shock as their boss fell to the floor. They had the message loud and clear.

The two men walked out to the truck, struggling under the weight of their radioactive load. "Why are you letting them live? They could raise the alarm?" said the boy.

"The tall ugly one is my cousin."

****

At the petrol station at Qa'im, just inside Iraq on the Syrian border, two ISIS fighters waited in a Ford Galaxy mini bus that was rapidly becoming hot and sticky inside. They had been there for some time, one of them got out and relieved himself. He returned to the bus, "Do you think they are coming? They are very late."

"We wait."

"We are very exposed here. The Security Forces could easily pick us up."

"We wait," said the other with finality.

So they waited and finally the convoy of heavy trucks came through the checkpoint at the border. They were escorted by guards travelling in lightly armoured vehicles. Scant attention was paid to the convoy and they were, more or less, just waved past by the Iraqis. The border was like a sieve and smugglers for the Government and the opposing factions traveled virtually unhindered between Iraq, Turkey and Syria. Trade between the three was probably more vigorous than before the conflict had started. The region had descended into total chaos. Fighters were going one way and insurgents the other, guns in, guns out, drugs and Jihadi brides were passing for good measure. The whole area was a complete security shambles.

The convoy pulled over to swap the escort for the next leg of the journey. The drivers got out of the assorted trucks and HGV's, relieved themselves, ate, faced towards Mecca and prayed. The occupants of the Galaxy joined them in prayers. By now a small fleet of trucks and cars had arrived in the area. It was apparent, that on crossing the border, the truck drivers all had small business ventures going with various locals smuggling items from one side of the border to the other. The gas station had descended into a mini bazaar.

It was a very simple matter for the mini bus occupants to help the driver of the truck carry the large box and place it in the rear of the Galaxy. "Sorry for the delay lads," said the driver "got held up on the road. It seems there was a change in the group that controlled a stretch of the highway. It took an age to sort out the bribe to allow us to pass. It cost me another eight hundred dollars to deliver your goods."

They knew that he was bumping the price up and they guessed he had probably paid a tenth of that. They were in no mood to haggle and gave him the extra. The driver was almost embarrassed by their lack of bargaining, but he, of course, accepted the extra cash.

The Ford Galaxy pulled away from the stop and headed south. If anyone had pointed a Geiger counter at it, they would have seen the needle go off the scale.

******

There were three bombings in Baghdad that day and over a hundred people were either dead or injured. The hospitals were struggling to cope with the injured and dying. ISIS was under pressure and they had been losing ground recently. They were stepping up their bombing campaign, part in retaliation, but also in order to let the World know they were still a force to be reckoned with.

The University was in a state of chaos. A targeted bomb had left the Campus in disarray. Students and staff were among the dead, dying and injured. Ambulances, security forces, police and militia were all engaged in the action. Chaos and panic had spread across the Campus.

The three ISIS members were looking for the Metallurgy Faculty and referring to a map of the building. Soon, they located the secure facility. Security today, however, was totally lacking following the carnage outside. The combination of suicide bombings and the random shooting into the crowd of students had made anyone, with the slightest instinct of self–preservation, get well clear of the Campus. They marched along the corridor to the store of radioactive material and literally, just blew the doors off with a small, plastic explosive charge. They walked back out with a holdall stuffed with the deadly radioactive material, got in a car and drove off. ISIS had just gone nuclear.

Chapter 2

The rain dripped through the hole in the sun awning into the bucket placed on the terrace by the bar owner. There was a large puddle where the bucket had over spilled. A young couple made a dash for the café, the male, wearing flips flops, slipped and nearly fell. The female was more sure footed and reached their table in a less dramatic fashion.

The tables and chairs on the terrace outside the Terminus Café, were a random collection of plastic, cane and metal. They had obviously been collected and replaced over the years and were a total mismatch. The Patron came out and, nearly slipping and falling himself, emptied the bucket that was filling at such a rapid rate in the downpour, served little purpose. Tim looked at the sagging awning, the red stripes faded into the greying white background and wondered, given that the rip in the awning was no bigger than six or seven centimetres, why the owner had not applied a piece of duct tape. Perhaps duct tape was rare in France, or perhaps the owners just could not be bothered and accepted the heyday of the Terminus Café, located directly opposite Menton railway station, had long since passed.

Tim sat with his back to the Café with the open glass door to his right giving him a clear view of the terrace, the station car park and the coming and goings of those entering and leaving the railway station entrance. He stirred his double espresso, three sugars, too many. He kept meaning to cut down, but somehow, forgot each time he put spoon to cup.

To his left there sat the cowboys. Two almost identically dressed men with white beards, stained orange with nicotine. They wore black leather sleeveless jerkins, white stained T shirts and black faded leather cowboy hats with large cross stitching on the brims and crowns. Their sleeping bags and Worldly possessions were stacked under cover in a shop doorway to the left of the Café. Their hands shook as they lifted their coffee to their lips, which the patron's wife had placed on the table in front of them a moment before. They were obviously regulars. The dog that emerged from the Café ran to greet them and was instantly scooped up onto one of their laps by trembling hands.

On Tim's right was a large red and white bag on a chair. Beside it, on the table, were three further, smaller plastic carrier bags stuffed with old clothes. The owner appeared from the Café and stood by the bags. She was in her fifties, hair long and dirty. Her hands also trembled as she struggled to raise a cup to her lips. The drug and alcohol abuse were etched in her face and thin body. She was dressed in flimsy, floral patterned beach trousers, a leopard blouse and a beige wrap around cardigan. Her feet were dirty, her toenails uncut and her toes forced over and under each other by the large bunions on the side of her, flip flop clad, feet. At some stage she must have had a life and obviously had loved her high heeled shoes. Tim imagined her as a young girl, dressed smartly, with her designer shoes and handbags, going to the Casino in Menton, or dancing in the night clubs. No longer desirable, broken and addicted, all her possessions in bags, she relied on the Terminus Café for her morning ablutions. She hopped nervously around the table, taking alternate sips of coffee and dragging on a roughly rolled cigarette that occasionally stuck to her lips.

Tim took another sip of his very sweet coffee and looked up to see a group of four men running from a black van to the cover of the terrace. There was more slipping and sliding on the treacherous wet tiles before they reached the safety of the chairs and sat at a table. The bucket was now overflowing, as the rain continued to pour down. Thunder could be heard in the distance. The patron appeared with croissants and coffees and greeted the arrivals. Their jackets showed them to be railway workers. A fifth man dashed in and joined them and was greeted loudly by his co-workers.

So far, not one of the Café's customers fitted the bill of the man he was expecting to meet. He ordered another espresso and again put too much sugar in it. Tim, whose real name was Anthony Burr, had acquired the nick-name from his schoolmates. They had been unable to resist the opportunity for the joke, a "chip off the old block, timber," so the name stuck with him. He had been waiting at the Café for nearly an hour so far. Tim was forty one and looked out of place as he sat in the rain in the faded establishment. His clothes were a cut far above those of the other customers and his well-groomed appearance made him conspicuously noticeable. He felt uncomfortable.

This weekend had certainly not turned out as expected. He had anticipated spending a jolly few days at the Hotel Lewes in Monaco, watching the Grand Prix and perhaps getting a bit of sun. Today was race day and he had his place reserved on a nice yacht facing the track. Instead, he was sat, in probably the grubbiest café in the Cote D'Azure, doing someone else's job in the rain.

He had joined the civil service after he left Selwyn, Cambridge. He had done well enough, with a two one degree, to get a job in the Home Office. After a few years he was transferred to help out the long suffering Ambassador in Paris, where he would use his knowledge of foreign affairs to brief him daily with what was happening in the World. Technically, he was employed as an intelligence officer. Sounded like a spy but, in reality, he read the local papers, checked the briefings from the various government departments and made sure the Ambassador had a clear picture of the current situation and a clear understanding of what the current policy thinking was. After working in Thames House for a couple of years, he finally got Paris and was on this beano in Monaco. Along with the Ambassador, staff, some trade delegation chaps, he had managed to wangle the invite for himself to watch the Grand Prix, from a yacht booked by the Turkish trade delegation, in the Marina.

A note had been passed to the Ambassador's aide and as they had no one spare, here he was sat in the rain, waiting to meet a contact who, presumably, had a bit of inside information on trade or some such thing, while everyone else was tucking into a champagne breakfast on a luxury yacht.

He looked at his watch. His contact was late. The couple had left and the railway workers were making their way across the car park to the station. The itinerant cowboys appeared to be texting. How odd the World was. Nowhere to sleep, but you had a mobile phone. The table on the other side of the door was now occupied by a black man with a large suitcase on wheels, not his contact, a traveller perhaps? Not so, he clearly was the supply centre for the horde of beach hawkers that sold cheap goods on the beaches. He was approached by further Africans and goods were swapped around and money changed hands. The bag lady was looking at a mobile phone on offer from a beach trader, but there was still no sign of his contact.

The rain had stopped, the hills beyond were still bathed in a grey mist and rain and the distant sound of thunder could still be heard. He looked at his phone, checking the Grand Prix update. It was raining in Mote Carlo as well and the start of the race was under threat. He had now waited for nearly an hour and half. Enough he thought and made his way inside to settle up.

No one was to be seen, clearly service was not a priority at the Terminus Café. He heard voices from a side room. He stood and waited for a while. In the end, with no sign of anyone, he made his way towards the sound. He stood in the doorway. The family were sat around a table, covered with a red and white plastic check table cloth, having their breakfast. He stood. They looked quizzically at him. "The bill," he said.

Reluctantly, the wife got to her feet and making him feel as though he was a nuisance by being a paying customer, she walked to the bar.. He followed her. His French was poor, GCSE standard. He could not understand the number being requested and pointed to the till which should have displayed the amount or printed off a bill but did neither. This caused a blast of French. The till was clearly not in the regular habit of being used. Cash in hand was the order of the day here. He removed ten euros and offered it to her. Success, change and he tipped her fifty cents. He had to admit, that although not salubrious, the Terminus Café was value for money.

He turned to leave, feeling that the morning had been a waste of time and effort. "Monsieur pour vous?" she handed him an envelope from behind the bar. It was addressed "L'homme Angletere," vague but effective.

Outside, he pulled out the note and read." Hotel Belgique, Room 15, Rue de la Gare. After 10, the concierge goes at 9. Code 8476, Stereogram." His heart sank. He would have to come back tonight. This was not the fun break he had hoped for.

He realised he was already in the Rue de la Gare. He glanced down the road and could clearly see the Hotel Belgique. He considered the note. "Who calls them self Stereogram?" he said to himself as he made his way across the car park to the railway station.

The rain had stopped in Menton, at least. He had purchased a return ticket in Monaco, so he went straight to the platform. The train was on time, but crowded with race goers. The journey took ten minutes with two stops. Then the problems began. He knew he needed to buy his ticket now for his trip back to Menton that evening. The queues would be huge after the race. Leaving the train, he tried to make his way to the main ticket concourse, but was blocked by a group of race officials. The crowds were being controlled by the seat numbers to their positions around the circuit. He tried to explain that he wished only to purchase a ticket, but that was clearly not in the remit of the marshals who ushered him off in the opposite direction. The station, he had to admit, was spectacular, clad in pink marble and spotlessly clean. Despite its architecture and splendour, he was losing interest in its elegance as he walked the whole underground route to end up at the other end of the town.

The streets were packed with race goers, street traders and race officials marshaling the pedestrians. Everywhere was jammed and everyone, it appeared, was going in the opposite direction to him. The rain had started again and was tipping down. He was very wet and fed up by the time he finally made it back to the station ticket office. He finally bought his return ticket to Menton. It was nearly two o'clock by the time he returned to the hotel to find everyone had left for the yacht. A pass to allow him access to the Marina had been left behind the desk, but he would have to get himself there. The Ambassador and the rest of the party had a nice escorted limo drive. He, on the other hand, would be back in the crowd, marshalled and wet. He set off with his recent purchase of a grey and white souvenir Monaco umbrella.

Chapter 3

Berat woke to the smell of tea, simit bread and the sound of hammering downstairs. His Mother was busy in the room next door, where she and his Father slept and where they all ate and watched television. Although it was just seven in the morning, he knew his Father had been up for hours working in the shop downstairs.

The whole flat smelt of leather, always of leather. They lived above his Father's cobblers shop. By the time he and his brothers were fed in the morning and went down the stairs to go to school, his Father would be busy at work. Piles of shoes were stacked up in the house, in the shop or outside waiting in pairs on the pavement, either for sale or collection. His Father was not the only cobbler in the street. The whole street up and down had the scene repeated. His trip anywhere, always started by passing between piles of footwear on the pavement surrounding his home in either direction.

His friends Emir and Ahmet were waiting to walk to school with him, He made his way past shoes and said goodbye to his Father who sat on the floor with a bradawl in his hand and a shoe on the last. His Father always said, "Work hard and get an education. You don't want to end up doing this all your life."

He took on board what his Father had said. So he had worked hard and had an education. Now a grown man, he sat on the wall overlooking the Bosphorus. The noise of the traffic on the road behind him was deafening. Vehicles of all shapes, sizes and ages streamed past, many blasting thick plumes of oil burning smoke. He suspected that Turkish emissions laws for vehicles, like many other laws, were not strictly enforced. In some ways the Country had come a long way since he was a child, in others it was going backwards. Ataturk, the Father of the modern Country, had created a secular government distinct from the religion. For a while, with the exception of the odd military coup, it had functioned, but now the State was more repressive and fundamentalism was on the rise.

Stretching in front of him was the sea, glistening with patches of oil and pollution. The oil tankers lined up to enter the Bosphorus, the twenty mile long north-south strait that joins the Sea of Marmara to the Black Sea and separates Europe and Asia. The ships were so large and appeared so close that you felt you could reach out and touch them. They seemed like toy boats in a bath. He had grown up with this sight all his life, but it still continued to captivate him. Now, in his mid-thirties, working as a civil servant, he longed for the simplicity in his life as it had been as a child, playing in the streets of Istanbul.

The Bosporus was just a part of his everyday life, from childhood he had taken it for granted. He remembered, as he gazed on the comings and goings of the vast ships, the day he had gone to University. His Father had gathered the whole family, brothers, cousins, aunts, uncles and friends to celebrate. His Father's pride was so great that he felt the burden to succeed weighing on him. He set himself to nothing but study and achievement. He did succeed, a first class degree followed by a masters and a well-paid secure job in government. He had taken extra language courses and spoke perfect French and English. He now travelled frequently around the World, acting as translator for the great and good in government and commerce. He knew that the English name Bosphorus came from the Greek bous, meaning cow and poros, meaning crossing, cow crossing. The legend went that Zeus had an affair with Io. When his wife Hera got wind of it she turned Io in a cow and created a horsefly to sting her bottom. It hurt so much that Io, the now cow, jumped across the strait.

He smiled to himself as he thought of cows jumping over the queue of tankers waiting to move oil around the Globe. His smile faded as he thought of Emir and Ahmet, brothers. He had grown up with them, shared school, fights, and sexual adventures. They were more like his own brothers or his family than friends. Their lives, of course, had diverged, he to University while they had remained in the grubby backstreets of Istanbul scraping a living as best they could. They were still close, but their life experiences were separated by a gulf wider than the Bosporus. He knew that, with their increasing frustrations and poverty, they had become more and more fundamentalist in their beliefs.

Behind him he could hear the call to prayers ringing out across the city. It was not that he was a bad Muslim, it was that he was more tolerant and inclined to live and let live. He valued peace. He had seen enough suffering acting as a translator around the Globe to know that the World did not need a helping hand down the road to more pain. Ahmet, the younger of the two brothers, had first become involved actively with the Fundamentalist Brotherhood when he was in his late teens. Like all young men, he had imagined himself the hero, fighting for truth and Allah, saving the poor, fighting the good fight. Berat reflected, as a child watching the old kids' television programs of jousting knights rescuing damsels, he had also seen its appeal. He knew all young boys yearned to be heroes and brave and the Muslim Brotherhood movement offered the chance to fight the corrupt and gain glory.

Ahmet started attending the more hard-core seminars held at the Mosques, meeting with other frustrated young men and searching the internet for like-minded individuals. It was not long before his brother Emir was being drawn into the more radical form of Islam as well. Now in their thirties, they wanted change. The idea of secular government was an insult to them, their beliefs and above all, to Allah. A trip to Syria had hardened their resolve and they were committed to the cause. Berat, to an extent, humoured them, not wishing to lose touch with that part of his life and his roots in the streets of Istanbul. He had been guilty, to an extent, of letting them think he was right there with them.

Celik, his wife was their younger sister. Berat had known her as the little pest that the three of them had teased as children. That had changed one summer when he came back from University. They fell in love and married. She was a good wife but shared many of her brothers' beliefs. Berat knew that, as her husband, she respected his wishes and never voiced her opinions to his more secular colleagues they mixed with.

As he sat watching the sun coming down and turning the sky bright red, yellow and lavender, it seemed to him that it was like an omen. His World was changing, he had not asked for it but it was. He now had choices, choices that Allah should ask no man to make.

Berat had been excited at being part of the delegation going to Monte Carlo. Of course, French was his specialist language and he would head the team of four translators working with him. It was a chance to influence the British. They all knew their support was key to Turkey's entry into the European Union. He knew that every opportunity would be taken to polish their record on human rights, their commitment to fighting terrorism and to demonstrate their commitment to the West.

He was finalising the details with his team when Yosuf had asked him to step into his office. Berat immediately sensed that this was not the usual, checking on final details, type of meeting.

"Take a seat," Yosuf commanded. This was unusual, Yosuf was not a command type of person. Berat feared he had made an error and was to be hauled over the coals. "There is a problem, a big problem," Berat feared that his job was on the line as Yosuf continued.

"You are married to Celik and she has two brothers, does she not, Emir and Ahmet?" he did not pause for a reply." "As I said, there is a problem." He seemed to struggle to find the words to continue. The word problem hung in the air. He took a deep breath. "They are to be arrested."

Berat's mouth hung open in surprise, "Arrested, for what."

"Security matters"

"My wife?"

"She will be fine, do not worry on that account; I have vouched for you both. I told them I know you to be a loyal servant of the State and totally dependable."

At that moment Berat realised his suspicions of Yosuf were well founded. He had always suspected that there was far more to Yosuf's role than just head of the Foreign Office translation department. He now realised, in that role, Yosuf could travel around and liaise with his Country's espionage resources globally. He had worked with him for nearly seven years and this confirmed that he was definitely part of Counter Intelligence. With hindsight, Berat began to see historic events in a new light, burglaries, disappearances and killings fell into focus. He was not just a translator. He was part of the cover for the State to carry out what it needed to do.

"You realise you must not warn them, nor tell your wife, don't you?"

Berat nodded, but he knew that he would and that decision would change his life for ever.

Yosuf knew he should not have warned Berat, but he was fundamentally a decent man. Turkey was such a contradiction. The State was becoming more oppressive, reversing women's rights and curtailing the media, on the other hand it was fighting a campaign against ISIS and terrorism. He knew Berat was a good man and he genuinely hoped that with this warning, he would keep himself and his wife well clear of her radical brothers. His hopes were to be in vain.

Berat knew he would betray his boss, even as he was warned to stay silent, but he also knew he could not stand by and not warn his wife. He left the office and changing trams had made his way to the Grand Bazaar. He knew this could be a trap to test his loyalty and feared that he may be followed. He hoped that the most crowded area in Istanbul would give him a chance of not being observed by anyone sent to follow him. He mingled in the crowds, stopped, doubled back and hoped he had avoided a tail if there had been one. He entered the phone shop.

Berat had purchased the cell phone for cash with credit on it. Sent the text to Celik warning her, with instructions for her to destroy her phone and dispose of the sim card. All the authorities could trace then would be an anonymous text from an unregistered phone, but the content of the message could not be retrieved. Berat removed the sim from his new phone, pulled out the battery and dumped it.

Celik ran down the road looking from side to side. She knew people were watching her. She was sweating and panicking. She ran as fast as she could. The text had been clear "Your brothers are to be arrested for terrorism. Do not use any phones, they are tapped, warn them and destroy evidence."

Her lungs hurt as she ran up the winding staircase to the flat where her brothers were. She banged on the door. The door opened onto a normal scene. "Grand Theft Auto" was paused on the PlayStation, they had been drinking coke and eating crisps as they played.

"What's all this noise," asked Ahmet, standing in the doorway dressed in shorts. "Is there a fire?" She pushed past into the room.

"The police are coming and you must get rid of any incriminating evidence, do not use the phones." The look of panic was in their eyes. Frantic activity began as she left.

"Take this. Someone will contact you for it," Emir pushed a memory stick into her hand. She kissed her brothers and ran again. She was a street away when she heard the sirens.

When Berat arrived home he found Celik upset and distraught. She had followed his instruction to the letter. "They were arrested. I warned them and they gave me this." she gave him the memory stick. Berat plugged it into his computer, but could make no sense of its contents. He did know, however, what was on it should be in the hands of the State, but handing it over would put the final nail in the coffin of his own wife and her family. He could destroy it and not warn anyone, but he was sure that that would result in the deaths of innocents in their hundreds or more. The alternative of giving it to ISIS, when they contacted Celik, which they surely would, was also not an option.

Chapter 4

The race was due to start at four and it rained like it can only rain on the Mediterranean Coast. Warm and wet, it continued to rain and then, as if on cue, the rain eased and the race started under the safety car. It did not take long before the drivers became bored with driving in convoy so they decided that the conditions were good enough and the air was filled with the full glorious roar of Mercedes, McLaren, Renault and Ferrari. It was loud, Formula 1 loud. The cars were a blur as they passed in front of the yacht. The Lady Heloise, moored in Monaco, was a hundred million dollars' worth of some one's toy that looked like it had never set to sea in its life.

She was moored at a beautiful location on the straight with bends visible at both ends. The Marshals in their red overalls lined the track along the quayside in front of them. The lower deck had been laid out as a dance and buffet area, while the upper decks were for the Brits and drinkers whose glasses were constantly filled with champagne. The lower deck was crowded with beautiful people. A video operator filmed the guests from every angle with a camera suspended from a gimbal and a stills photographer snapped incessantly. A black girl, with almost an afro, in a very flimsy bright yellow dress and her white friend in a bikini made sure they danced their way into every shot. Other young girls were scattered around like cushions to add to the décor.

Tim positioned himself on the top deck and watched the cars going round the track behind the safety car, He then watched as Verstappen crashed and his Red Bull car was hoisted clear off the track by a crane, as the race continued under the virtual safety car. The virtual safety car required the cars not to overtake and follow the car in front at a non-race pace until the green flag sign was illuminated, signaling full racing was to recommence. As the race resumed, Tim was approached by the Ambassador.

"Ah you made it? Sorry we couldn't hang on for you, but as you know there is the schedule to keep to in all these affairs." He smiled broadly as he spoke. He had a full face, a face that seemed to ooze affability and understanding and eyes that focussed on whomever he was speaking to, letting you know that you had his full, undivided attention. It made no difference if you were the cleaner or the Premier of China, that face was always totally absorbed and interested in what you had to say. He did actually sound genuinely sorry for leaving Tim to wander through the crowds in the pouring rain while he was chauffeured in luxury.

"No problem. I enjoyed the walk and needed the exercise," Tim lied.

Jason Delonge was your typical old Etonian, totally confident, comfortable in every situation and knew anybody who was worth knowing, added to that, he had obtained the trendy must have Philosophy, Politics and Economics first from Oxford, suits from Dege and Skinner in Saville Row and was set for all steam ahead in the diplomatic World of today.

Tim knew that Jason was actually brilliant at his job, but couldn't help feeling a bit irritated by how easy it had come to him. Tim also had his suits made by Nick at Dege and Skinner, but he always felt like he did not quite belong there and somehow the suits seemed to look better on the Ambassador. In truth the Ambassador had run to a paunch while Tim worked out in the gym daily and had practised martial arts since joining the society at Cambridge.

The conversation could only take part in short bursts in the brief relative quiet when the cars were not flying past. "How did your trip to Menton go?

"Nobody turned up," he picked the wrong moment to reply. Clearly the Ambassador had not heard a word, but by force of habit, seemed fully engaged.

"That's good then. You can sort it out on Monday with the naughty boys." He wandered off heading towards the decorations dancing on the lower deck. Tim turned his attention back to the Grand Prix. The naughty boys referenced were the attachés assigned by MI6. The spies every embassy had.

"Hi." He turned to see an oriental girl in her mid-twenties with a massive straw hat garnished with flowers, wearing what appeared to be a recreation of a Mary Quant lace mini dress. His eyes were automatically drawn to her chest where her nipples were clearly visible through the gaps in the crocheted work. She was stunning, too young, too obviously on the make but very pleasing to look at.

"Hello, are you enjoying the race?" he asked.

The roar of the engines did not make conversation easy. He did establish that she was planning to be an actress, model or something in PR and that she knew a great deal about shoes and fashion. Clearly they had a great deal in common. He liked the look of her body and she liked his career prospects and the fact he was divorced with no children.

He had met his wife at University and they moved in together for the second year in a house share. The third year at Selwyn meant he had a room in the College, so there had been a brief separation before they reunited in and moved to London. In hindsight, he probably would have done worse on his course if he had lived with her in the third year. She obtained her first without breaking sweat. She had the brains. They married when they got to thirty and planned on children.

Then it all started to go wrong. Lisa's career went cosmic. A whole new world, she was a banker, then a fund manager. He saw the change in her. There was nothing he could do. He knew he was boring, pedestrian, and irrelevant. She was dynamic, energised and a winner. They were no longer the people they were at Cambridge. They were now poles apart. The divorce had been quick, more painless for him than for her. But life goes on.

He looked at the girl standing beside him and decided that life was not going to go on with her that day. He made his excuses and watched as Roseberg lost pole allowing Hamilton to go on to win.

In the office on the lower deck, the translators, provided by the Turks, were lacking in co-ordination and leadership. Yosuf was furious. "Where the fuck is Berat?" He shouted at his aide.

Chapter 5

Booking the Hotel Belgique had taken Berat a few clicks the night before and there had been no queue at Mote Carlo for his return ticket to Menton. It was early Sunday morning and most of his colleagues would just be making their way down for breakfast. He made his way along the long marbled halls to platform two. The platform was virtually empty. He immediately spotted the Englishman from the British group waiting for the same train. He recognised him from the cocktail party on the Friday night and the qualifying session which they all watched from the Lady Heloise. They had not spoken, but he was pretty certain he would recognise him in turn.

He had not expected this turn of events. He, in no way wanted to be identified as the source of the information. Turkey was a member of NATO and shared intelligence with the other member States. One slip and his name would be out and the Turkish authorities would know that he had aided his brothers in-law.

He sat down on the benches that were positioned at intervals along the platform. Unlike most seating on station platforms, they did not face the rail track but were positioned at right angles facing the bench opposite. There was a middle aged man and a teenage girl sitting opposite him. They were very engrossed in each other. Berat now had his back to Tim.

Berat's mind raced. He needed to rid himself of the memory stick, memory sticks to be accurate. He had taken the precaution of copying the original. He could feel them like two enormous weights in his jacket pocket. In hindsight, his plan of meeting a British agent in a hotel room seemed a bit simplistic. Pass an anonymous note, meet a spy, dump the information and go home to a normal life. Now it seemed far more complicated. True, he wanted to prevent the deaths of innocent people at the hands of ISIS, but he did not want the source of the information traced back to him and his wife,

He jumped as a train rushed through the station without stopping, shaking him from his thoughts. His stomach churned with nerves and he felt himself sweating, despite the cool of the subterranean platform. He took several deep breaths in an attempt to calm himself. He needed to come up with an alternative plan that did not reveal him as the source and expose his links to his brothers in-law.

The Menton train pulled in on time. He remained seated and watched as Tim boarded the train. At the last instant he jumped up and also boarded. The journey was only around ten minutes with just two stops. As the train pulled into Menton station, he made sure to be by the doors. Pressing the button to open the doors, he hurried from the train and platform. On exiting the station he instantly saw the Café across the car park. From his visit to Google, he knew that the hotel Belgique was just a hundred metres past the Café on the road to its left.

There were a few diners in the dining room having breakfast, but no-one else to be seen in the Hotel Belgique. He had entered via a glass door into an outer lobby and then into what was the reception area. There was a desk with an open door to the right which led to the dining room. He looked on the reception counter for a bell or something. There were the usual brochures for things to do in the area and a note saying the desk was manned from seven to eleven in the morning and five till nine in the evening. In the dining a room a short black woman appeared carrying breakfasts and placed them on a diner's table.

She saw him "Just a moment," she called as she went behind the bar at the end of the dining room and began to operate the espresso machine. Coffee served she came to the desk. "You were due yesterday evening, two nights," she said.

"Delayed," he had booked for two nights so he would have the room available today. She gave him the key to room fifteen and the code to the front door, should he need to get in after nine in the evening. He paid in cash.

To the left of the desk was a grubby grey, marble spiral staircase. Room fifteen was on the second floor. The grout between the marble tiles on the steps was black and the handrail wobbled as he grabbed it walking upwards. The hotel had its location on its side, directly by the rail Station but very little else. It had been neglected for years. Probably the only time it even approached being full was during the Grand Prix. This was borne out by the diners, who either wore their supported teams logos and colours on their clothing or on their caps. He climbed the stairs to the first floor, paused on the landing and continued up to the top floor of the building.

Room fifteen had a double bed to the left as you entered and a single along the wall at the bottom. A small table, an old chair and a hang rail completed the furnishings. To the right there was a stud wall that didn't reach the ceiling. This contained the smallest basin, toilet and shower known to man. He sat on the chair and considered the turn of events. He placed the two memory sticks on the table. He felt relief at relinquishing them, even if he had only distanced himself from them by a few inches.

He slowly came to the outline of a plan. He looked around the room for a hiding place. He knew, the longer he had the sticks in his possession, the more he was, potentially, providing the smoking gun that would shoot his wife and her brothers. At that moment a train went by, causing the whole room to shake. It galvanised him. He looked around the room for a place to hide them. The usual suspects came to mind - bed, toilet cistern or stuck to the bottom of the table or the chair. All he considered too obvious. His eyes fell on the half closed shutters to the window at the bottom of the bed. Perhaps he should consider outside the room and not in it. He squeezed between the bottom of the bed and the second bed to the Juliet balcony and opened the shutters. He looked around the window opening and gingerly put one foot on the balcony, which he did not trust to support his weight. There was a crack just above his head. It would do. He pushed one stick in, one down one to go. He left leaving the room unlocked.

On his way down he noticed the old stereogram sitting on the mezzanine landing. It presumably had been part of the owners decorating theme, forties retro, or just left over tatty. It had a vase with a bunch of plastic flowers on it. Moving the flowers, he lifted the lid in the centre revealing the turn table. He put the stick on the table, put the lid down, replaced the vase and made his way down and out on to the Rue de la Gare.

Berat turned left as he exited the hotel into the pouring rain and entered the Terminus Café from the side entrance. He could see the Englishman through the glass window sitting on the terrace with his back to the bar. He bought a coffee and swiftly scribbled a note. He pointed out Tim to the owner, handed him the note and an extra ten euros and left. He knew he would have to meet the Englishman at some stage, explain all and trust that his identity would be kept secret.

He stood on the pavement wondering if the Englishman would spot him as he passed the Café and made his way across the car park to the station. While he hesitated, he became aware of the two strangers beside him before he actually saw them. "Stay calm, this is a gun you can feel."

Chapter 6

Celik had barely left her two brothers. There was a fire going in the waste bin and their computers lay smashed on the floor. The doors flew open and the room was filled with shouting bodies. "Get down, armed police, police, on the floor, hands behind your head."

The shouting continued as Emir and Ahmet had hoods placed over their heads, cuffed and were dragged from the building. They were bundled into the back of a van that then raced through the streets of Istanbul. The next twenty-four hours were a blur. No water, no food, no sleep and no toilet facilities. A plane and another van ride followed.

The hood was pulled off and the handcuffs removed. Emir found himself in a windowless cell with a single light bulb in the centre. The door slammed and he blinked his eyes, dazzled by the brightness, after hours of darkness. His lips were cracked through thirst, his skin hot and parchment like. His body was filthy. His own piss and shit were in his trousers and down his legs that had been rubbed raw through hours of being left sitting in his own excrement.

He noticed a jug of water in the corner on the concrete floor. It just stood there in the bare room. He half crawled and half staggered. Water had never tasted so good. He gulped it down. Too much, too quick, his stomach cramped, twisting like a knife. He vomited. Then more calmly he sipped at the water. Over the next few hours he was left alone, left to let the fear grow inside. The only sound was the occasional loud banging and screaming.

He examined his location. He touched the stained walls, scrutinising them closely and realising that the stains on the walls were blood. A few pictures, printed on a cheap printer on A4 paper were stuck with sticky tape to the walls. They showed men and women, mostly naked, all had brutally beaten, with broken limbs and smashed and bloody faces. The worm of fear grew.

He sat and waited and waited, the fear growing stronger inside him. He looked at the cracks in the plaster on the walls. His imagination and sleep deprivation causing him to see faces, monstrous faces, in the patterns in the plaster. Some seemed to be smiling, mocking him. He checked the thick wooden door with the stains, dirt and grime engrained in it. He looked for a source of light apart from the yellow dingy light suspended from the single strand of flex, He watched the cockroaches scratchily scamper to and fro, disappearing into cracks in the walls and floors and then reappearing from another. In the background was the constant sound of voices, sometimes raised then interrupted by violent shouting and then moans, wailing and screams. His mind began to take over and imaginings dominated, Nightmare scenarios filled his head, demons from hell, ripping dogs and the walking dead. Lack of food, sleep and isolation forced delirium to the fore.

How long, no way of telling, hours or minutes or day from night. He tried pacing, he tried sleeping, and he tried creating pictures of his family in his head. He tried reciting the Koran and placing his faith in the Prophet, "peace be upon him", but fear still predominated and the isolation continued. No contact, no input, nothing to feed the senses, just the background noise of pain and suffering.

The door slowly opened. Nothing dramatic, no slamming banging or the sudden rush of bodies or clatter, just a small crack that slowly widened. A large Arabic looking man dressed in combat trousers, heavy boots and a black round necked t-shirt lumbered in first. His beard was full, his hair cropped in military fashion. He was a huge man with thick, powerful arms, his neck short, set above massive shoulders. Emir knew that this man was battle harden and had not only seen death but had caused it on many occasions. This man followed orders and would never shirk his duty.

He was followed in by a much smaller man, a dapper man with neatly trimmed hair, a light blue shirt, slacks and slip-on beige shoes. He looked like he was off to the shopping mall or the cinema, or perhaps off to start his daily role as a school teacher. He carried a clip board. They both stood, briefly staring at him huddled in the corner of the room.

The smaller man spoke. He looked down at his clip board and then up at him. "Emir, you do seem to have put yourself in an awkward position. Don't you?" he paused and smiled. "Well I think I may be just the fellow to help you out. Of course, that rather depends if you can help me a little as well. You scratch my back and I will scratch yours"

"Where am I?" Emir found his voice came out as a trembling whisper. He knew he sounded like a whiney schoolgirl.

"I am not at all sure that is important, but in a spirit of the cooperation that I hope will exist between us, I will tell you this. We have a sort of agreement with the Government of your Country to undertake certain tasks. Think of it as outsourcing, a bit like moving the garbage or running a hospital. Yes that is it outsourcing. Your Government has outsourced, to us, the task of asking you some questions. You may ask why they don't do this themselves and I shall answer that question for you."

He paused and looked at Emir. "You do want to know why you have been outsourced, don't you? I am sure you do." answering his own question. "The Americans like to call it rendition, but I prefer the term outsourcing. So, we are recognised leaders in the field of information extraction. It is a simple process. Gather up the subject, in this case you and of course your brother, pop them on a plane to us and just like that we get you the answers you want. "

He continued, "You may ask what the advantage of this outsourcing is? Again in the spirit, of what I hope will become mutual cooperation, I shall answer that question. You can already see, I hope, what a reasonable man I am? Your Government, I might say, like many other Governments are, quite rightly, firm and staunch upholders of human rights and would under no circumstances use questionable interrogation practices. Turkey, like its allies the United Sates and the United Kingdom and the rest of Europe, which I might add some day hopes to join as a member of the European Union, all therefore do not carry out any such questionable practices. Of course, this would in the normal course of events make it harder and take longer to get answers from the bad men like you and your terrorist buddies."

"Now that both of us know where we stand, I should appreciate it if you would answer a few questions for me?"

Emir said nothing. The large fellow, despite his bulk, took a fast step across the cell and smashed his fist into the centre of his face. His nose cracked, his lips split and blood filled his mouth.

"I think it is important we develop a line of communication. I should appreciate it when I ask a question, that you have at least the good grace to answer. The first question I should like to ask is. Who are you working with?"

This time Emir received a kick to the stomach that forced all the air from his body. He gasped and doubled up and retched, only bringing up bile from a stomach that was completely empty.

"Oh Emir I can see that you are going to be one of those troublesome individuals who would like to experience a great deal of pain before they give me answers to my questions. Given that this is your preferred way for us to proceed, I think it is time that we went a little more high tech, rather than us having my friend here do all this manual stuff like punching and kicking. "

He banged on the door and another military clad figure pushed in a large cabinet on wheels. Emir looked at it. "This is an emergency power supply and you can up and down the voltage etc. state of the art and highly robust. And this is a cattle prod."

The door open again and a chair was brought in. "And this is for me to sit on," he smiled at his own joke. "And this is for you to sit on." This time a much more robust chair was wheeled in with wrist and ankle straps. "Please be so good as to remove your clothes."

Emir didn't move. He was dragged to his feet by the gorilla and stripped. He was dragged from the room and dumped in what passed for a shower where a hose pipe was pointed at him. The freezing cold water made him gasp and the power of the hose was such as to knock him from his feet. He was dragged back and strapped into the chair.

"Now, I hope you feel better after your bath and are sitting comfortably? You could save all this trouble if you just tell me all about it, a few names and the whereabouts of a certain memory stick." Emir said nothing.

Emir screamed. The prod had been first placed on his left nipple then his right. He knew he couldn't survive this for long. He cried, he pleaded, he screamed, but the pain kept on coming.

"I think the penis? Don't you? I am afraid this may affect your chances of having children. Well that is, if you live that is."

Emir passed out.

Emir had been moved while he was unconscious. He awoke to pain everywhere and his brother. This was a different cell, much bigger, with bright lights and more facilities. Water, electricity, a bath, not he guessed used for bathing, chains, hooks and pulleys hung from the ceiling. His brother, Ahmet, was a mess of blood, bruises and broken bones. He was barely conscious and was strapped upright to a large cross against the corner of the cell wall.

"Welcome back Emir" his interrogator spoke softly, as usual, as though they were just having a normal conversation over a cup of tea. "You see, I like to bring families back together," he paused so that Emir could take in the full implications of the sight in front of him.

He raised his hand and the ox, as Emir now thought of the big man who had tortured him for hours, went to the table and opened a box, paused and pulled out a scalpel. Without a word he approached his younger brother's naked body and lifted his penis clear of his scrotum. The knife began to cut into the flesh. One testicle was laid bare of the scrotum and the second revealed in like fashion. His brother was barley aware of what was happening as his testicles were popped, like peas from a pod, from their covering.

Emir heard his voice "Stop, Please stop. I will tell you."

"I knew we could do business, now let's begin. No time like the present, as time is pressing. Would you like something to eat and drink, perhaps, as we proceed?"

Chapter 7

Mehmet, deputy head of Turkish security, was aboard the Lady Heloise in Monte Carlo. He and his entourage were gathered in the private stateroom. The conversation was constantly interrupted by the roar of the cars. Mehmet sat at the head of the circular, glossy, rosewood table. "Where is he?"

The rest of the officials looked at each other nervously. Yosuf replied with some trepidation. "Gone, disappeared, he left early this morning and hasn't returned."

"Get out, all of you and ask Jason Delonge if he could spare me a few moments of his valuable time."

Jason arrived and he and Mehmet sat opposite each other. "How are you my friend?"

"Fine Mo and you?" asked Jason.

"I need a little help and I think you are the man to help," he paused to let Jason know that this was not a request but a demand.

"Of course."

"This morning I received news that an interpreter who works for us, has a certain something in his possession that we should like."

"I don't understand, what has your interpreter to do with me?"

"You will. His name is Berat and some associates of ours have been talking to his brothers in-law. These men are bad men, terrorists, members of ISIS and they gave Berat something which we should like back. A USB memory stick in fact and when we received this information we went and searched Berat's room at the hotel and it was not there, nor was he. We did not find the stick, but we did find an email to you."

Jason knew he had a problem. This was obviously something he had to hand over to British Intelligence and he could not hand it over to a Foreign Government. He also knew that Tim had failed to meet with this Berat and he did not have the stick in his possession as yet. "Why do you need it, surely you can let MI6 deal with it?"

"My Government wants the credit, you understand, for this. It would be a major coup for us in the fight against terror."

"I cannot help you," Jason got up to leave.

"Oh! But I think you can and you will." Mehmet turned the laptop round that had been facing him on the desk. There was a video image of Jason and the small boy with the big oval eyes.

Jason Delonge stared unbelieving at the screen as he had hoped never to see that face again. He thought back to that summer five years ago. He had not been surprised to receive the invite from Mo. They had been firm friends at University and they had travelled to North Africa together, smoking dope and buggering the young men during the summer recess. Of course, Jason had given up the dope, but not the buggery and was well on his way to a career as a diplomat. Mehmet Yildirim's, Mo's, career had also progressed since their time at University. He was looking forward to seeing his old friend again and there was always the opportunity to swap a bit of intelligence that had the potential to be helpful to both their careers. The plane touched down on time and with his diplomatic passport, Jason was soon sat comfortably in the back of the black Mercedes, sipping a glass of champagne, as the driver struggled with the traffic in Istanbul.

The villa was incredible, the automatic gates rolled open to reveal a sweeping cypress tree lined drive that wound its way to the house. Jason liked to describe the architecture as Middle East, over the top, bling. The big double doors were opened by the butler onto the marble clad vestibule with a double staircase curving upwards to the galleried landing. The biggest gold and crystal chandelier hung the full two stories from the domed ceiling that was panelled in decorative, painted glass. Even Jason had to admit this was bling on a whole new level. Every nook and cranny was stuffed with antique furniture, gold objects d'art and tapestry works. Even the old Sultans would have been given a run for their money in this place.

As is the nature of Turkish tradition, the house was more or less segregated between the public and the private. You did business in one and the family lived in the other. The house was arranged around a beautiful tiled, central square garden with a bubbling fountain that issued clear, sparkling water. Obviously, the owner did not feel the need to stick with any particular style of architecture and had not minded adding a bit of Moroccan into the mix. It was totally over the top, but, if not demonstrating the taste of the owner, it certainly demonstrated his wealth,

"Jason, so glad to see you," Mo crossed the thick pile of the traditionally patterned, hand woven carpet of the library. The walls lined with volume after volume of leather bound and hand tooled books, Light streamed in from an ornate window at the end with verses from the Koran etched around it.

"Mo. It has been too long. What a beautiful place." said Jason.

"Not mine old boy, a friend's. In fact there are a couple of people who I should like you to meet after you have had a wash and brush up. They will join us for diner. Just the usual business types looking for introductions in the UK and a nod of approval," Jason was not surprised, after all, there was no such thing as a free lunch.

Dinner was quite a formal affair. There were eighteen, including his host and himself, all men of wealth. The table was magnificent, gold cutlery, finest crystal and fine dining. "Mr Delonge," said the gentleman to his left. "I understand that you and Mehmet went to Oxford together?"

"We did indeed and Eton of course."

"The finest school in the world, I am hoping for my son also to go. Firm friendships are built on such experiences. Friendship is so important, don't you agree?" Jason agreed. "Such friendships last a lifetime and can be so helpful in meeting the right people, the right circle, and the right network."

He paused and stared at Jason, trying to gauge his state of receptiveness. Jason smiled and nodded knowingly. This encouraged him to continue. "Perhaps after we have sampled this delicious meal you, me and a few of my colleagues could discuss some sort of arrangement?"

Jason decided to not let this go all one sided and he knew enough to make the play a little difficult. It would all add to the price at the end of it, he did not want to appear to be too cheap. "What sort of arrangement?"

"Oh nothing formal, of course, we respect your position and neutrality, but perhaps there are areas of mutual benefit we could explore."

The meal had been sumptuous and Jason could not help but notice how the small boys, aged no more than nine or ten, had scurried around helping the serving staff. As he settled in an armchair in the library, a dark haired boy with large oval eyes and long eye lashes passed him a glass of Remy Martin from a silver tray held by the butler. He smiled and looked away shyly.

The discussions went very well and Jason had added significantly to his annual income and would, in return, provide ad-hoc consultancy to his new business acquaintances. He settled back in the armchair. The guests having left, he and Mo sat facing each other. "Do you remember those weeks in Morocco?" asked Mo.

"Never to be forgotten. Good to be young with no commitments."

"Ah yes, commitments, they do have a habit of cutting down life's pleasures." He beckoned the boy, who had served Jason earlier and gently stroked his head. "It is a shame these commitments." He waved the boy away. "Goodnight, I think."

Jason made his way to his suite of rooms. A bathroom in gold and marble, a dressing room, a lounge with a bar, a television the size of a cinema screen and a huge bed completed the accommodation. He discarded his clothes and headed for the shower. The water was warm and ran down his body. He wondered if there might be a porn channel on the television. He felt his penis begin to harden. He stroked it up and down in the shower using the soap as lube. He continued rubbing gently up and down until it was fully erect. "A nice wank over a bit of porn on the TV and he would get a good night's sleep," he thought as he made his way from the bathroom.

At first he was startled, there was someone in the room and his heart jumped. Sitting on the bed was the small boy with the oval eyes and soft olive coloured skin. He looked tiny sat in the middle of the huge bed naked.

The screen on Mehmet's laptop now displayed what the secret camera had caught in that room five years ago.

Chapter 8

Yosuf had seen that look in Mehmet's eyes once or twice before. Mehmet, he knew was a fanatic in his own way but not a religious zealot, nor a man of principle. He was, in fact, more of a sadist with an incurable drive to inflict pain. The job he had allowed him full licence to his passions, including torture, rape, paedophilia and murder. He felt his stomach knot and the hairs on the back of his neck rise as he met Mehmet's stare.

He knew he was dead. It was only a question of how and when and how much pain was to come. On balance, Yosuf thought that he would be allowed to travel back to Turkey so he could quietly disappear. Killing him here in France could bring messy complications, as the French were not that keen on people dumping bodies along the Cote D'Azure.

He had worked with Berat for six or seven years. He knew him. He was a good man, a decent man, who worked hard at his job and a good Muslim. When he heard that Berat's brothers in-law were to be arrested and were involved with ISIS, he just wanted to warn Berat so he could make sure that he and Celik distanced themselves and cleaned their house, so to speak, to double check they had nothing, nothing at all to link them to the terrorists. He should have known better, for the very reasons he had warned him.

He had been stupid and with hindsight he should have known that Berat would, being the man he was, try and protect his family. Now it was all too late, events had led him and Berat, both of them, to certain imprisonment or death. His mind raced. "What were his options?"

He knew he had but one choice, run. He hurried to the cabin set aside at the rear of the Yacht for communications. The amount of equipment was small, a powerful computer, a printer and a guard on the door. They could encrypt and send secure messages and scramble the phone, allowing them to communicate with home with relative immunity from being listened to or hacked. The cabin had been swept for listening devices so it also afforded the opportunity for very private conversations. The cabin also acted as a secure location for their confidential possessions, bags, laptops and files, the things you would not leave in a hotel room.

As he descended to the secure cabin, he considered Berat's actions. He realised, that once Berat's wife had warned her brothers and become involved by taking the evidence against them he, Berat, being a decent man, had needed to do something. He should have destroyed the evidence, but his conscience would not let him. He could not hand it over to Mehmet as that would have been tantamount to handing his wife over for torture and providing a death warrant for her brothers. Knowing that he had a piece of evidence that could potentially save countless lives, Berat had wanted to get that information into the hands of someone who would use it, but not against his wife and family. So he had contacted the British. He had not foreseen that his brother in-law would have cracked under torture and given up his sister. Nor could he have foreseen that the Brit he contacted would be a paedophile buddy of Mehmet's. In fact, as soon as Celik became involved, it had only been a matter of time before he was in the firing line. Yosuf was also pretty damn sure that ISIS by would be sniffing him out soon as well. Turkish security leaked like a sieve. There was a great deal of support for a return to fundamentalism all across society and Government Departments were not isolated from society as a whole.

The guard smiled broadly at Yosuf, as he recognised him. They had travelled all over together and were friends, "How's the race going?"

"Hamilton has the lead and provided nothing goes wrong with his car he should take the win."

"You have all the luck, pretty women and fast cars. I just get to stand down here watching the luggage," he opened the door for Yosuf.

He entered and closed the door behind him. He had, at the bottom of his heart, known it might always have come to this. He had rehearsed it a thousand times in his head. Planned every move, but had never really expected it to become a reality. His hands trembled as he picked up the oversized bag. It was the type that accountants and lawyers used to carry their clients documents. Black, sturdy and leather clad, it was a cross between a big box and a carry-on luggage bag. It bore the diplomatic emblem and seal. These bags either travelled with their owners at all times, with the capability to be handcuffed to them, or they travelled in the hold of a plane in large, sealed, metal boxes. In any event, it was part of the diplomatic mission and immune from customs or any other form of border scrutiny. Guns, drugs and even people had been transported using this convention.

As Yosuf had risen in the ranks, he had become more and more aware of how perilous a career could be in a Country that seemed to be going backwards on human rights. He had started to slip things in his bag over the years. It had become a full flight and survival kit. Passports, money, IDs, it had built up over the years. He took his bag and tapped on the door to be let out, "You are not the only one to miss the race, the lowlier of us have work still to do," he quipped with the guard as he left.

There would be no going back, he knew that, he also knew that going back to Turkey would be injurious to his health and potentially, fatal. The party was now in full swing. A black girl and

45

her friend were doing a striptease for the lads and he knew a couple of the prostitutes were conducting a gangbang in a cabin in the bowels of the boat. All good fun to lubricate the spirit of international friendship,

He had one small matter he wanted to satisfy himself on before he went. He spotted Ahmed, the gofer, with the other porters and valets congregated in a small group watching the two strippers, now rubbing and playing with each other, putting on the lesbian finale to their show before they moved to join the other prostitutes to do their fucking duty downstairs. He carefully pushed his bag under the buffet table and made his way over to the group.

"Met," he said, gesturing for him to come over to him. He was known to all and referred to as "Met the bag," for obvious reasons. "Can you tell me something?" he asked. Met nodded in response "Did you load up the British contingent at the hotel and ship them down here?"

"Yes, I always take personal charge of the foreigners, better to have a fuck up with your own group than balls up the guests transport, why? Is there a problem?"

"No, no problem, but tell me, did they all make the limos?"

Met rummaged through his pockets and pulled out a piece of paper. "My list, it is like a school trip. I count them on the way here and count them out on the way back. That way I don't leave any lying around anywhere." He smiled as he looked down at his list.

"Only one, Anthony Burr, made his own way here."

"Thank you," he said. Yosuf knew who Anthony Burr was and decided to have a wander around and take a look for him, before discreetly picking his moment and disappearing

Chapter 9

The ISIS banner, with its bold lettering in white on its black background, hung from the wall. The hooded figure moved from the camera's field of vision revealing the tableau behind. The computer screen filled as the web cam was moved in closer

"Do you recognise that cunt?"

The screen showed a close up of the female genitalia. A hand appeared from out of shot and roughly began to probe the labia, seeking the entry. The camera pulled back unsteadily, showing more of the scene.

The lower half a naked woman's body was stretched across a table, her legs tied to the legs of the table exposing the hair of her pubic region, the hooded figure probing and pulling roughly. She was completely naked. The hooded figure held his erect penis in his other hand, he was rubbing it vigorously.

The camera widened its angle further and her naked body, in its entirety, was exposed, her breast slipping slightly to the side of her chest. One was being fondled by a second hooded male, also exposing his erect penis. The camera hovered above her chest.

"Infidel whore," was written across her chest and stomach in Arabic.

"Fuck the whore," the voice said. "Such bitches are there to serve you, the sons of Jihad. She is not human. She is scum that floats to the surface when confronted by the truths of Islam." The rant continued in the same vain, becoming almost hysterical as she was fucked. She was pounded with no regard for her body, "Fuck the whore and fuck her hard."

Celik had just popped down to the shops when the van stopped in the street. Before she had a chance to respond, she had been dragged into the back, gagged and hooded. No one reported it. Then the hell had begun. She had been taken to this filthy room and raped hour after hour. "Filthy whore, fuck the whore, fuck the slut's cunt, fuck her arse." It continued and continued. She screamed, she pleaded, she bled and her body tore.

"See how your slut wife enjoys it." Rough hands forced Berat to look at the screen. Berat had been marched back to room fifteen in the Hotel Belgique. He was pinned to the chair by two individuals with a knife to his throat. Tears ran down his cheeks as he struggled frantically to free himself. He was no match for his captors. He could not cry out, his mouth stuffed with the towel from the bathroom. He slumped forward. He had lost the will to fight. He could not bear to watch his beautiful wife being used like a piece of meat any longer. He looked up at his captors, pleading, a broken man.

His captor removed the gag, "well?

He gasped in air, "On the balcony, in the crack above the window."

His tormentor moved to the balcony and pushed the shutters open and looked above him. There it was. "It is here," he confirmed to his companions. The knife was drawn across Berat's throat and there was a gasp and a cough as the three left room fifteen.

Chapter 10

The station at Monte Carlo was packed. The race had finished and the big rush was on to get away. Tim was glad he had purchased a return ticket to Menton when he had returned earlier that day. The ticket inspectors were ferocious, making sure no one entered the platforms without a ticket. There would be no fare dodging today. Tim struggled to board the train, in which every bit of space was occupied, as it pulled from the Station.

He was a little fed up with the situation. The rest of the party would be taking a limo to the hotel where a sumptuous dinner had been laid on. He hoped he would be able to deal with this bit of nonsense quickly and get back to join in the festivities.

He crossed the station car park at Menton and noticed that the bag lady was still wandering the terrace and the cowboys were still occupying the corner table. He wondered if they had been there all day, or if they had come and gone. He passed the Terminus Café and continued to the Hotel Belgique.

The glass door was closed, there was no sign of the concierge. Tim approached the keypad and looking at the note passed to him that morning by the patron of the Terminus Café, he entered the numbers. There was a click and he pushed the door open. The lobby was empty as he climbed the grubby, spiral staircase. He looked at the room numbers on the first floor and realised he had a further flight of stairs to ascend.

The door to room fifteen was before him. He knocked but there was no response. He knocked again. He was now feeling intensely irritated, thinking that the whole day had been a waste of time. In frustration, he tried the handle. The door opened. He entered.

The room was in semi-darkness, with shutters closed, as he peered into the room, he struggled to see inside as his eyes adapted. At first he thought the room empty then the figure came into view, sat at the table. "Hello?" he called.

Berat would never answer again and when Tim entered and saw his corpse, blind panic set in. He was frozen and stood motionless, taking in the awful sight before him. Then his brain raced back into gear. What should he do, call the police or get back to the delegation? He made a decision. He would get back to Monte Carlo, re-join the delegation and then contact the police. That would, at least, give him the full protection of the diplomatic process.

He began to descend passing the retro stereogram. He retraced his steps and calming himself he focussed. The note had mentioned stereogram, not the code name of the writer then, but a real stereogram. He looked at it. He saw the dust had been disturbed where the vase had been moved. He wanted to get out of there, but he steadied himself. After all, he had been sent to collect something and so he should at least make an effort. It did not take him long to find the memory stick. He pocketed it.

Tim closed door to the Hotel Belgique and he stepped onto the pavement. He tried to look normal. He was aware that, the more normal he decided to act, the more abnormal he felt himself acting. He thought everyone was watching him. The rain had started as the race had finished in Monte Carlo and now it was pouring here in Menton. The sky was grey and the far mountains were obscured by the mist and descending night. He looked up and down the road, He was trying to control his breathing and stay calm. Nothing had prepared him for what had confronted him in room fifteen. He saw no one, but he was half expecting the police to appear from nowhere and sweep him up.

He started to walk up the street past the Café to the station. As he drew level with the side entrance to the Café the door opened and a man blocked his route. "Mr Burr, a moment please," Tim stopped dead.

Yosuf stood in front of him, Tim struggled for a moment and then recognition crept in. He knew this man to be a translator with the Turkish Delegation. His brain raced, run, stay, was he in danger? As if reading his mind, Yosuf said "My name is Yosuf and I mean you no harm, Please talk with me. I assure you I merely wish to talk."

Something in Yosuf's manner convinced Tim to listen to him, or perhaps it was the shock, or the fact that he knew him by sight from the Yacht. In any event, he followed him to the back of the Café.

"How did you get here," Tim asked.

"I followed you. I was on the station at Monte Carlo, you came onto the platform and I saw you. I merely got off when you got off and watched you go into that hotel. I was hoping you would lead me to a friend and colleague. I believe he was to meet you?"

Tim felt the panic rise. This man was looking for the man whom he had left for dead no more than two minutes ago. He struggled for words. What could he say? Yosuf interrupted before he had time to respond. "Did you meet?"

The rain began to fall harder. Tim nodded. He didn't know why he answered but he did. Yosuf gestured for Tim to follow him inside. They sat at a table hidden from the street, coffee was ordered and put in front of them. "I need to warn my colleague Berat," continued Yosuf. "He is in terrible trouble. I was hoping when I followed you that you would lead me to him. Please tell me if he was in the hotel? Is he still there?"

"He is dead. He was dead when I got to the room."

Confusion, fear and shock all progressed across Yosuf's face. "That cannot be?" There had not been time for Turkish intelligence to locate him and they could not have followed Tim as Berat was dead before he got there. In any event, they would not have risked murder on foreign soil. They merely had to wait for his return and arrest him. At that point they could consider their options.

Yosuf calmed himself and lent forward. Everything had changed from when he spotted Tim on the platform and followed him. His first intention had been to follow him from the boat, but he had not seen him aboard. He had decided to take the only course of action open to him and that was to flee before Mehmet acted against him. He had his escape kit, in the form of his large bag with him and the rail ticket to Italy was in his pocket, when he had seen Tim on the platform. On the spur of the moment he had decided to follow him and try to warn Berat.

Now, Berat was dead. "Do you have the memory stick? Do not fear, I do not want it but if you do, I think you should be very careful indeed."

Tim considered the matter. He felt that this man was not out to hurt him and, in a strange way, knew that he was sad to hear that his friend was dead. "Why should I be careful?"

"I think, as the Americans say, we are both "dead men walking". You have something my Government wants and wants badly. Worse, or not much worse, it is something ISIS wants. I, Mr Burr, am on the run from my Government at this precise moment and I am in no doubt I will disappear quietly should they catch up with me. You think you can take what you have and give it to your Mr Delonge? I will warn you that this will not result in a good outcome. In fact, by doing so you would be guaranteeing your own death I fear."

Tim was struggling to understand. Yosuf continued, "I have no interest in the matter but having failed Berat, for that is the name of the man you have just left in that hotel, I will give you this small amount of advice. Your Mr Delonge is under an obligation to Mehmet and he must help him get the object you have. You, my friend, will be an obstacle to keeping Mr. Delonge safe. The solution, I fear, will be your disappearance from this Earth."

"Who killed your friend?"

"I cannot be sure but clearly not my Government, they merely had to wait for you to return with the package, silence you and take care of Berat at the time and place of their choosing and deal with me at their leisure. I fear it was ISIS and if you have the stick, it will not be long before they are looking for you. Turkish security is very leaky and infiltrated with sympathisers."

Tim took a sip of the now tepid coffee as he allowed the events of the last few moments to sink in. "What does your Mehmet have on Jason Delonge?" Yosuf told him exactly what kind of man his boss was. Tim was feeling as if the World he thought he knew never really existed. He involuntarily put his hand to his pocket and felt the memory stick.

Yosuf noticed his action." You are holding your death warrant, but perhaps with some luck we may turn what you hold into our salvation. Come we must go."

He stood up and picked up his big, black bag. Tim followed. What choice did he have?

Chapter 11

The Thames was glistening in the sunlight, the slight film of oil on the surface of the green water reflected back the colours of the rainbow. The cruise boats could be seen going back and forth under Westminster Bridge. The tourists were busily snapping pictures of themselves and the Palace of Westminster. The loudspeaker systems on the boats could clearly be heard, their running commentaries describing the sights, the Houses of Parliament, the Abbey and Big Ben.

Jason Delonge stood on the terrace overlooking the river, a pink gin in his hand. The terrace was crowded with MPs, Lords and visitors. It was a clear, sunny day and everyone took the chance to grab a break at lunchtime and get a bit of fresh air. He had changed his plans and after a bit of string pulling managed to get a flight from Nice to London City airport that Monday morning. He had been scheduled to return to the Paris Embassy, but the events in Monte Carlo had necessitated the change.

He sipped the gin, bitter sweet in his mouth and nodded to the odd face he recognised. He had been waiting for nearly an hour, the Minister he wished to speak to was a busy man, He waited patiently, watching the traffic back up on the bridge. Big Ben struck and on the last strike, as though by design or coincidence, a voice spoke behind him. "Jason, it is good to see you."

The speaker was a slim man with greying hair, with not a single one of those hairs out of place. His grey, lightweight, woollen suit was immaculately tailored to fit his slim frame, nails manicured and

54

the white silk shirt was finished with a deep blue tie, signalling his party allegiance. Jason proffered his hand and a polite handshake was exchanged. Although Terrance Mailer had professed his pleasure at seeing Jason, his manner contradicted his verbal statement.

"I do apologise, but I have a very tight schedule and can only spare you a little time," he continued.

"I think we need to find somewhere a little less public," Jason said.

This was greeted with a look of reluctance on the others behalf. "I really do not have much time."

"Find it," Jason's voice held a note of firmness that shook the other, "unless you want the World to know about some of the parties we go to."

Mailer was visibly taken aback and glanced around him to check no one was in ear shot. "Have you taken leave of your senses?" Jason said nothing and Mailer let out a sigh of resignation. "Follow me."

Given the exterior grandeur of the Houses of Parliament, the Minister's office was surprisingly small and cluttered. The building was not in a good state of repair and it was clear that remedial work was desperately required. To date, all Governments had been reluctant to spend the billion or so to restore the building and find an alternative for the five years or more that it would take to bring the whole thing into the modern digital age. Jason sat himself in the shabby, leather chair. Mailer sat himself on the edge of the desk, having made space by pushing a pile of papers to one side.

"Well, what is this all about?"

Jason relayed the events of his weekend in Monaco. He finished his tale by saying. "If I do not aid our Turkish Intelligence friend Mehmet in recovering the missing details of the ISIS plot, I will be joining the list of paedophiles prosecuted by the police under operation Yew Tree. And more to the point, I do not intend going down alone."

Mailer's face drained of colour. He knew that the threat was not idle. The scandal would bring down a large number of current and past leading figures in the political elite. "I understand. Well what's to be done old boy?"

"Firstly, we need to locate Tim Burr. You can get that done. It is your area of remit. Get your lads in MI6 to trace his phone, credit cards or whatever but find him."

Mailer nodded, "What about this Yosuf. Are the Turks sure that he and Burr are together?"

"It is the only explanation as to why Tim did not return to the hotel yesterday. I expected him to come back, give me the memory stick if he had it and I would have quietly handed it over to the Turks. Now we have a dead man in Menton and two missing employees, Tim and Yosuf. The Turks will obviously be hunting for their man."

"What happens when we locate them?"

"You may not need to find Tim of course, he may well turn up at MI5 or MI6 and hand over the goods. However, that does leave us with the prospect of you me and our little group facing a long stint in the clink on bread and water."

"So we find him," Mailer paused "And?"

"We let the Turks deal with it. They get the kudos of stopping an ISIS plot and Tim and Yosuf quietly disappear."

****

Berat's assassins sat in the small room above the carpet shop in Istanbul. Downstairs the tourist were being served free tea and being sold overpriced carpets by the shopkeeper. The atmosphere was tense. "This is a copy." The memory stick was thrown on the table between them.

"How were we to know?"

"Your instructions were precise, you had the make and there was a small mark you were to check. You were too keen to kill my friend."

The three fidgeted nervously as the silence continued. Finally, it was broken. "Fortunately for you three, there is a second chance for you to serve the Cause. Our brother, working in Turkish intelligence, has informed us that two men are being sought."

He threw the two photos of Tim and Yosuf on the table. "Find them, kill them and destroy the original. We will be updated as to their whereabouts as and when the Turks find them."

Chapter 12

Tim looked out of the window of the bus as it drove up the Rhone Valley. He felt tired and stiff. Sleep had been difficult with the movement of the vehicle, the cramped seat and the concern he felt as to this undertaking. He knew that his only hope was to make it to London and hand the memory stick to someone other than Jason. The problem was getting to London alive and avoiding leaving a trail. Yosuf seemed to have the knowledge in that area. He, also like Tim, had a vested interest in avoiding Mehmet and Jason and he hoped that with the help of British Intelligence, he would be able to start a new life in the UK with a new identity.

Under Yosuf's instruction, they had placed their mobile phones in padded envelopes and posted them to different locations before boarding a bus for Nice. There, they then transferred to the bus heading to Paris. The rain finally stopped as the bus arrived at Lyon. It slowly made its way over the bridge, through the rush hour chaos outside. They were tired and hungry.

"We need to get off here and take the train. This is too slow," said Yosuf. They made their way across the road through the line of traffic and sat in a café. After a coffee, Tim felt more awake. He felt the tension of being hunted and the uncertainty of being with a stranger that he had met only hours before and in whom, it would appear, he would have to trust if he wanted to stay alive.

"I feared that this day would come and I should have to flee. Turkey is difficult," said Yosuf, "Freedoms you take for granted are not that easily come by for us. The press, television, the internet, they are all censured. We say we fight terrorism than brand the Kurds terrorists so we can have the excuse to terrorise them. We help people to cross to Syria to join ISIS while we do a deal with the European Union to block the refugees fleeing the conflict. We want to join the EU, but we do not make the slightest effort to comply with the requirements of membership, a fucked up policy."

Tim looked at him as he took another sip of coffee. "So you prepared?"

"I prepared. Fake passport, currency and unregistered phones all are in my big black bag. I have seen too many disappearances in my line of work, too many so called accidents and I really do not want to be an accident and if I am to disappear, I decided I would be the one to do the vanishing trick."

They paid and left. After a two hour train journey they arrived at the Gare de Lyon in Paris, then a trip on the Metro to the Place du Concorde, followed by a walk to the Place du Madeleine and the hotel Madeleine. The room was adequate but sparsely furnished.

"You need to stay here," said Yosuf. Tim looked hesitant. "You have to trust me or go it alone."

In the street, Yosuf made his way to a supermarket, part of the Geant Casino chain and bought a mobile phone for cash. Further along the street, he entered another shop and purchased another. By the time he arrived at the metro he had four unregistered phones. He made a phone call and removed the sim card, smashed the phone and discarded it in a bin. His journey to the Paris suburbs involved a change of trains before he entered the Turkish café in the mostly immigrant quarter of the City. He drew no attention from the other occupants who were engaged in playing backgammon and sipping the bitter sweet, thick as mud coffee. He ordered coffee and sat at a table with a backgammon board in front of him. He drank his coffee, a taste of home and sipped the glass of water that accompanied it. He took the Turkish language newspaper from a rack and settled down.

The man who joined him was small with very dark skin. He had a small beard, unusual for a Turk who in the main preferred the clean shaven look. The facial hair served a purpose in that it coved a long scar that ran under his chin. "Cousin," he smiled at Yosuf as he sat opposite. In truth, they were not cousins, but they were vaguely related and had been close as children. Yosuf had not seen Osman since he had had a run in with the Turkish police.

"How is business? Are you still in the same line of work?"

Osman smiled "What is a poor man to do? What else do I know?"

"I am need of your services."

"I am happy to help. I shall be eternally in your debt, for without you my home would be in a nice Turkish jail. What can I do?"

Osman had been rounded up as part of a Turkish "look tough" policy for the benefit of the West on people smuggling. Of course, the real people who benefited and lined their pockets were higher up the food chain, the politicians, police and Government officials, who were not affected by the so called crackdown. Yosuf had used a few contacts and a few bribes to get him released and a visa to France but not before he had a taste of police hospitality that resulted in the scar and the new beard.

"I and a friend need to get to England without going through the usual channels."

"Consider it done my friend," beamed Osman.

Tim woke with a start as the door to the room opened. He sat bolt upright. "It is only me." Yosuf entered the room and placed a plastic bag on the table." Food," he announced.

Tim had not realised how hungry he was as he took a bite from the baguette filled with ham and cheese. "I fear I am not a very good Muslim," said Yosuf, as he ate his. "Everything is arranged. We travel tonight. A car will pick us up outside the hotel and take us to the coast."

Chapter 13

Rome, four in the morning, there was the sound of the clatter of glass bottles on glass bottles as the garbage carts collected the empties from the myriad of small bars and restaurants throughout the city. The clanking of empty bottles rose to a crescendo as the carts rolled over a roughly cobbled section of road. The locals were used to the din and quietly slept on, while visitors in their hotel beds always woke up with a start to the racket.

The street, on which the hotel Bella Roma sat, was unusually crowded for the time of morning. Two men are on the corner, one is a doorman and one a road sweeper who had been sweeping the same patch for the last twenty minutes A signal was given and the two men entered the hotel and approached the night porter.

Lisbon, two hours earlier and apart from the sound of a dog barking or a drunken argument in the distance, the Beacon Hotel was getting the same treatment. Two men entered and approached the desk.

At both locations the photos, obtained from their passports, of Yosuf and Tim were shown and the register checked.

"Fuck," said Mailer. Jason looked across the desk at him as he put the phone down. He had scurried to Mailer's office in Whitehall an hour earlier, "Get over here. We have a hit on Tim's phone." He had said.

"Well?" said Jason.

"Red herring, he posted his phone to a hotel in Rome. Clever, I suppose. Not helpful, but clever. Yosuf's, the Turkish chap's phone, turned up in Lisbon."

"It does tell us that it is now highly probable that he and Yosuf are together, as both the letters containing the phones were postmarked in Menton. We must assume that our Mr. Burr is now much more of a problem than he was. This Yosuf is trained and tracking them and containing the problem will not be simple.

"So where the fuck are they now?"

****

Traffic on the Perepherique, the ring road around Paris, was moving at a snail's pace. Tim and Yosuf sat in the back of the Renault as their driver negotiated the necessary lane changes to get them on the right road to the coast of France. They had been in heavy traffic for nearly two hours and they had only reached Charles de Gaulle airport. The planes could be seen on the airport apron waiting to take off. Their journey would not be the thirty or forty minute hop to London by plane, but considerably more arduous and lengthy.

The driver spoke. Yosuf immediately recognised him as Kurdish in origin. "You are to take this package with you and deliver it to the address written on the piece of paper. Please remember the address and contact number now and then throw the paper from the car. The other items in the bag are a gift from Osman. He felt that they might be useful to you." He took a holdall from the front seat and passed it back to Tim.

Tim was surprised at the weight of the bag, he guessed it to be well over twenty kilograms. He unzipped it and looked in. There were ten sealed packets wrapped in a layer of duct tape. He showed the contents to Yosuf.

"Seems like Osman has moved on from people smuggling," Yosuf said, as he recognised the bound blocks of heroin. The Turks were long established in the heroin trade into the United Kingdom. Prior to the year two thousand, most of the heroin originated from the area known as the Golden Triangle, centred on Thailand, Vietnam and surrounding areas. Now its production was centred in Afghanistan in the area referred to as the Golden Crescent. Iraq and Pakistan were the main routes out and onward via the Turks into the United Kingdom.

It was a lot of the drug and Tim looked at Yosuf feeling a wave of fear run through him. Yosuf seemed unconcerned at the prospect of spending a long time in prison for drug smuggling. Yosuf, of course, had rationalised the situation and on balance caught with drugs or no drugs was a minor issue, as the outcome of being caught would be the same, death and the only difference would be the location, in a French prison or a Turkish prison. On balance the French prison would be far more comfortable.

Tim reached in further and felt round the side of the blocks of heroin. He withdrew his hand holding a gun. He was stunned and Yosuf, seeing the gun, reached across and took it from him before he shot himself or anybody else by accident.

Yosuf looked at the gun. He was familiar with it. "A Makarov," he said, checking that the gun was empty. The Makarov had been introduced by the Russians in the early nineteen fifties and was basically an enlarged version of the Walther PP. It had a detachable clip loaded with eight .9mm Makarov cartridges. Tim pulled a second Makarov from the holdall along with the ammunition clips and a box of shells.

The driver spoke, "Osman would like you to have them as a present. A personal thank you he said, for past services."

Yosuf placed the guns and ammunition in his big black bag. "I will show you how to use these later," he said to Tim.

Turning his attention to the driver, he spoke. What is your name?" he asked conversationally. Tim was taken aback by the casualness of the whole thing. He was now a drug smuggler and had a gun and Yosuf had taken this in his stride, without even a sign of emotion. Tim was beginning to understand that his partner was used to this as a matter of course and that he was going to be on a steep learning curve if he were to get through this in one piece.

"They call me Ali the Kurd, but they usually just say, the Kurd."

Yosuf smiled and the conversation continued. The Kurd was just another displaced person from that region of the World. His family and where he lived, had been hit by all sides, persecuted by the Turks and Iraqis and in conflict with ISIS. Ali was earning his living as a driver for the drug smugglers.

The Perepherique gave way to the A26 motorway and the signpost to Calais. They turned off the Motorway and the Renault headed to Arras. The countryside reminded Tim of the West Country in England. The roads were straighter and the farmsteads were clearly French in design, but it was a distinct change from the Mediterranean where he had been the previous day. It was late afternoon when they arrived in Berk Plage.

There were the usual seaside attractions, a small children's carrousel was circling with little cars and horses and the odd smiling child while music played from the speakers, a crazy golf course, seaside shops and of course, the almost deserted beach. The Kurd pulled the Renault up in the car park by the carrousel.

"You need to take a fishing trip. Tell the skipper you love fishing in the Seine. Good Luck." With those words the Kurd drove off. Tim, carrying a bag full of heroin and Yosuf carrying his big black bag, now with a small arsenal added to its contents, headed to the small boat

Chapter 14

ISIS had no conflict in dealing heroin having the dual benefit as a source of funding for the Jihad and the corruption of the West. The partnership with the Turks was beneficial to both. The Turks had a virtual monopoly on the supply to the United Kingdom and ISIS offered good protection to the poppy growers of the Golden Crescent. It had only been a matter of time before the supporters of ISIS in France responded to the appeal on their many websites for information on the travelling Turk and Englishman.

The three ISIS assassins had not taken long to get from Menton via Nice to Paris and they now entered the café where Osman was indulging his passion for backgammon. They moved to the table where he sat and stood in front of him. Osman ignored them, sipped his thick sweet coffee and rolled the dice.

The smallest of the three, short but clearly very muscular under his poorly fitting jacket and white shirt, swept the back gammon set across the table and sent it crashing to the floor. Osman's opponent rose and moved away from the conflict. The other two ISIS strongmen moved round the table and flanked Osman, who took another sip of coffee.

The leader of the hit squad pulled a large knife from his pocket.

His friends stepped closer to crowd Osman. "Don't fuck with us," he said. "I need information, now where are they."

Osman looked up and spoke, "I suggest you leave now, you are interrupting my game."

The two men either side grabbed Osman's arms and forced him down into his seat. There was a series of clicks, like beetles scuttling across a tiled floor. The three became aware of the silence in the café. The two men holding him released their grip and lowered their arms to their sides. They stared at the café patrons. The small man turned to see a room full of guns pointed at them and he let go of the knife.

Osman rose and lent across the table, his face inches from his would be assailants. "Fuck off cunts," he said, "don't come to my house with your fucking threats. You count for sod all here. We run things here, not you. Piss off back to your fucking camels and tents in the shit hole you live in."

He sat down "Can I get some more coffee?"

He looked up and addressed his would be intimidators. "Now," he shouted "we don't want the hassle of cleaning your brains off the walls."

Ali, the Kurd, sitting in Osman's Mercedes watched as the band of three entered then left the café. He watched as they walked down the road. He started the engine and the car moved forward. He pulled up alongside them as they contemplated their next move. "Gentlemen, may I offer you a lift," he said.

******

The small boat had made Tim feel quite nauseous and he was glad when he and Yosuf boarded the larger fishing vessel as it headed out into the Channel. They lay in the bunks, sleeping as the boat began to trawl for fish off the south coast of England. The boat continued to follow its usual fishing routine. The crew worked efficiently, using the winches and ropes to catch the fish along the coast.

The fishing continued all night and they joined the crew for breakfast in the galley. The crew made no contact and said nothing. They were being handsomely paid to smuggle immigrants from France to England and wanted to know nothing beyond that. The demand was so high that the fishing was now merely a by-product of the people smuggling business.

"Time to go," the skipper said.

Tim looked at Yosuf, concerned. They were, after all, still miles from land. "Just a moment," said Yosuf, "I just need to use the john." Without waiting for a reply, he stood up and taking his big black bag, he headed for the toilet, He closed the door and removed the Makarov from the bag and pulled out the clip. It was empty. He opened the box of cartridges and checked them. The Makarov, notionally, took a .9mm shell, but the Russians measured the bullets slightly differently and consequently the ammunition for these vintage weapons was different from the standard. The box of cartridges was Makarov and matched the guns. Yosuf was satisfied and loaded both clips into the guns. He then put a gun in each of the outside pockets of his jacket. He left the safety on the gun in his left pocket and exited the toilet carrying his bag in his left hand and kept his right hand in his pocket holding the loaded gun with the safety off.

The skipper led them up onto the deck. Alongside and lower than them was moored another boat. It was wide and fairly squared nosed with a large cabin with a canopy that extended over the aft deck. Two men wearing large aprons and Wellington boots stood on deck. Lobster pots were stacked at the rear of the boat and two large barrels, one full of lobsters the other empty sat on the deck. Their bags were attached to a line and lowered down to the fishermen below.

Yosuf replaced the safety catch on the gun and took his hand from his pocket. "These gentlemen will take you on the rest of your journey, farewell," said the skipper. Tim and Yosuf scrambled down the rope ladder onto the deck of the lobster boat and were told to go below and stay out of sight.

Tim had thought the fishing boat from France slow, but it was a greyhound in comparison to the tortoise of the boat they were now on. It moved slowly along the south coast of England, rising and falling in the swell. It was not long before Tim had made several trips to the toilet to rid himself of the contents of his stomach.

The captain stayed in the wheel house, guiding the boat to its destination, while the sole crew member sat on deck. He took one lobster at a time from the barrel and after measuring it secured its claw by winding a thick rubber band around them. To aid in this, the band was first stretched open using a specially adapted tool which allowed the band to be neatly fitted over the pincers.

"It seems to me that smuggling people or drugs into Britain is not the most complicated of exercises," said Tim.

"Too much coast, that's the problem with islands," smiled Yosuf. He and Tim were beginning to develop a bond. In a way, Yosuf felt that he was atoning for his friend Berat's death at the hands of ISIS by helping this Englishman. In any event, he was beginning to like Tim and his slightly stuffy English manners.

It was mid-morning when the boat approached Eastbourne harbour. For once the sun was out and shinning on the Sovereign Harbour development. The harbour was an artificial one and was not at the juncture of a river entering the sea. It had been carved out by developers and the marina, flats, and shops had been constructed. The boat passed the old Redoubt on its portside as it followed the buoys in the dredged channel to the lock. There were a series of these redoubt fortresses along this stretch of coast and most had been adapted to serve as tourist attractions, housing museums and exhibitions. Two seals basked on the mud, lazily watching the boat as it entered the lock.

They waited in the lock as the water level rose. The top of the lock was lined with people out for a stroll. They leaned over and watched the water as it flowed in. The fishing boat rose slowly until the water levels matched and the gates opened allowing them to sail into the harbour

The fishing dock was under a bridge and to the left as they entered. The captain contacted the bridge keeper on the radio and the bridge was raised. Tim could see the pedestrians waiting for the bridge to be lowered so they could continue their promenades as they sailed under it. The boat pulled into the quay and the crewman tied off.

There was only one other fishing boat moored and the crew had clearly departed. The area alongside the boats was littered with ropes, fishing pots and nets. They stepped ashore. The captain pointed "Over there, past the gym is the shopping centre, buses and taxis."

Having made their farewells, they headed in the direction indicated to them.

They were in England.

Chapter 15

Osman had received feedback and was pleased that his cargo had reached England. Of course, getting the drugs to the UK was only the first part of a complex chain that would lead to the drugs getting into the hands of the junkies. The heroin he had shipped was virtually pure and any addict injecting it would be sure to overdose. By the time it was for sale on the streets it would be about thirty per cent heroin.

His bulk customers in London had a sleek operation. When they got the heroine they would cut it with paracetamol, reducing it down to about seventy percent. The drugs were then repackaged and sold on to the big players up and down the UK at about twice the price Osman had sold it to them for. The logistics of moving the drugs around the Country was a serious transportation operation in itself. The cars and vans used to transport the dugs had to be constantly changed. The UK has the most surveillance cameras in the World per head of population and the vast majority of road side cameras were linked to the police's ANPR system, Automatic Number Plate Recognition and the majority of the police cars also had the system installed. Once a car had been flagged up as a possible drug use vehicle, say through a routine traffic stop, it was of no further value. They were constantly buying and selling cars through auctions.

When the product reached Manchester or any other big city, it was then cut further, adding to the profit margin and broken into smaller packets for the local dealers, who would probably dilute the product again before selling it onto the street dealers.

Osman was glad he had been forced out of the people smuggling trade. The agreement between Turkey and the European Union, whereby they, in effect, agreed to stop the migrants leaving Turkey and house them in camps, had killed the trade. While it lasted, the immigrant trade had caused a mini economic boom in certain areas of the country. He would charge one to two thousand dollars per passenger to get from the Turkish mainland to a Greek island and this money flowed in part into the local economy.

For example, the sales of rigid hull inflatable boats had allowed manufactures around Izmir, a large town near the coast, to grow exponentially. He had himself been responsible for buying three or four boats a month from one manufacturer alone, Northern Cross boats. The deal with the EU had slowed down the domestic trade, but the cheaper cost of production had, with the initial impetus of the people smuggling, allowed the boat builders the opportunity to get into the international leisure market. Osman still kept in contact with his old boat supplier at Northern Cross and had been surprised to learn that they had an order for over fifty boats, from Iraq of all places.

He stepped from his bathroom, wrapped in a towel, looked round his bedroom and took a moment to reflect. Not bad he thought for a Turkish peasant brought up without a pot to piss in. His villa on the outskirts of Paris had a further five, sumptuously furnished, bedrooms, a home cinema, pool, a tennis court and three acres of land. The detached garage housed his car collection. A Ferrari and a Bentley were among its contents. Yes, he was glad he had been forced to change direction. The heroin trade was far more profitable.

He walked into the wardrobe, which housed his collection of shoes and suits. His shirts were neatly folded in drawers along the walls. He selected one of the Armani suits and matched shirt, tie and shoes to his choice. Osman was not for the understated and a bejewelled Rolex was on one wrist and a thick gold linked bracelet was on the other. He was a great believer in the maxim, "if you've got it, flaunt it."

Ali the Kurd had asked for the night off. This was a rare occurrence, so Osman had kindly let the man take the time off. He decided he would drive himself and take the 360 Ferrari, although it was over 12 years old, it was still a head turner.

He had dinner booked at a Michelin starred restaurant on the Rue de Maxim and a hot blonde lined up as a companion. A club, then back to his flat in central Paris. He checked his watch and then checked himself in the mirror. Looking at his watch, he saw that he was in good time to collect his companion.

Ali the Kurd had taken the Ferrari from the garage, washed it and parked it on the drive in front of the villa. Osman checked his appearance one more time in the mirror and picked the car keys up from the side table as he left.

Despite its age, the car smelt of new leather. He checked the adjustment of the wing mirrors and had one final look in the rear view mirror to check his appearance.

The explosion was massive, destroying not only all trace of the Ferrari and Osman, but demolishing half the front of his beautiful villa.

****

The bus pulled slowly out of the station in the centre of Paris and headed east. The traffic was heavy as usual and the bus crowded. Migrant works travelled from the poorer countries of the European Union and the buses were their means of transport. Coming or going to look for work, every penny counted as they sent money home to their families. They travelled for days moving where the work was.

Ali the Kurd was going home. He had not seen his wife for six years. His son had only been a month old when he had left. He had left the Turkish controlled area where he was treated like scum and discriminated against and persecuted at every turn, to find a better life west. Hoping to move his family to join him, he had tried to work, but he could not get asylum status so he had no means of working legally. The only work he could get was for the Turks. He hated them and their drug money, but he had no choice and at least his family had money that he sent home each month.

He was excited and he could picture his beautiful wife in his mind's eye. He could smell the scent of her hair and imagined the soft caress of her touch. So long he had been alone, but now, in a few days, he would see the smile on her face when he returned. He would be able to hold his son and daughter in his arms again after all this time. He was coming back a rich man. In the rucksack was the fifty thousand euros the three ISIS goons had arranged for him to have for the service he had afforded them. He told ISIS of Tim and Yosuf's travel plans to England and the bomb had been surprising easily to install in the Ferrari.

******

The City Jet plane taxied along the runway at London City airport. The three ISIS hitmen had secured three seats together and were all trying to get a glimpse of London as the plane came into land. The flight from Orly airport in Paris had taken under an hour. They were excited as none of them had been to London before.

They only had cabin baggage and were soon outside the airport. The largest of the three lit a cigarette and took a deep draught. A horn tooted and a taxi pulled up in front of them. The driver wearing the taqiyah, the Muslim cap opened the boot for them and they put their bags in. They sat in the car.

"Put the fag out mate," said the driver in a north London accent as they moved off. "It's illegal to smoke in a cab." The three looked at each other and smiled. The cigarette was thrown from the window.

*****

Mailer studied the report from special branch. He had to call in a lot of favours, in a lot of areas, before this turned up. Following the fruitless raids in Italy and Portugal in the vain attempt to apprehend Tim, he had to resort to the intelligence gathering community. He knew he was pushing his luck and exceeding his Ministerial Brief, but he had no choice as his secret needed to remain just that, a secret.

The report was from the Drug Squad of the London Metropolitan Police, gathering evidence on the heroin trade in the Capital. The link between drug money and terrorist funding was well established and MI5, along with all the other arms of the security agencies, kept a watching brief on the activity. The Met had an undercover policeman in place and he had reported back discussions among the traffickers of an English man and a Turk who were bringing in the next shipment. The Drug Squad were attempting to locate the drugs and the couriers who had entered the country in the last twenty four hours, but they did know that, in all probability, the drugs would be delivered, ultimately, to a location in North London. So it was just a matter of maintaining surveillance on that location and being patient.

It was too much of a coincidence Mailer thought. The drugs were of no concern to him, he needed the memory stick to get that scumbag Mehmet and that idiot Jason Delonge out of his life. He knew he would have to take a risk and step further over the line, he had no choice. He dialled a number and spoke to MI6, to a friend who had as much to lose as he and Jason. When he put down the receiver, he was assured that MI6 would now be running the investigation and the Met would be politely removed from it. In fact, MI6 would ensure that the matter disappeared, leaving the Turkish Secret Service with a clear field.

He phoned Mehmet, "We have your target," and gave him the address where Tim and Yosuf would be making the heroin delivery at some point.

Chapter 16

The room, although basic, was quite pleasant on the seafront at Eastbourne and they could see the Pier and the sea from their window. "Do you know they call this place God's waiting room?" Tim said. Yosuf looked bemused. "The old people all come here to retire," he explained.

"Right," Yosuf smiled. "English humour."

They had walked from the boat to the shopping centre. Trips to Asda, Matalan and T K Max had seen them wearing new clothes, carrying two unregistered mobile phones each and wheeling two nice bags containing the contents of Yosuf's black bag, twenty kilos of heroin, some clothes, bathroom essentials and a laptop computer. They had taken the bus to the Pier and checked into the hotel.

The laptop came to life and after about an hour of downloading updates and other routine maintenance, the machine was ready for the off.

"It will probably be encrypted," said Yosuf, as he put the memory stick in the USB port.

"Or not," said Tim, as the files popped up on the screen.

They opened the files and read them. "Well I cannot make any sense of it. Can you?"

"Not really. They seem to be insurance contracts."

What is DWT?"

He googled it. "That is not much help; doing weird things, driving while texting: death weasel tech and down with tyranny."

"It is to do with ship insurance. Try putting in marine DWT."

"Ah, here it is deadweight tonnage. A measure of the mass a ship can carry."

"We are out of our depth..."

"Another English joke?" asked Yosuf.

"The pun was not intended, but we do need some professional help as to what this means."

"Do you know someone who can help us?"

"Actually, against the odds, I do, but it will not be fun for me. My ex-wife's husband is an insurance underwriter."

"Phone her."

"I will. Don't rush me. I need to mentally prepare for such an event. She talks to me as though I am something she stepped on and needs to scrape off her shoe"

"Will she help though?"

"Oh yes, it will give her the chance to show me her stinking rich, successful husband and reinforce the fact that I am a total waste of space," said Tim.

"Well, you can't argue with that," said Yosuf.

Tim glowered at Yosuf, who smiled innocently back. "I am getting the hang of this famous British sense of humour. Don't you agree?"

"Lisa?"

"Tony"

"How are you?" Tim asked.

"I am fine and you?"

"Perfectly fit."

"Ok we've done the health check. What do you want?"

It had not taken long to get the pleasantries over. "I need a bit of advice ..."

"I have some. Get a personality and a bit of ambition, anything else?"

"Very funny, it's a technical matter. I need John to give me some guidance on insurance matters. Could you ring him and prepare the ground. I know it is a big ask, but it is for my job, you know, British trade and I need to be sure I have the facts right?"

"He is very busy you know?"

John was known in the insurance market as Mr. Midas as he had the golden touch. He made consistent underwriting profits year on year. "I appreciate that, but he would be helping my understanding of matters for the Ambassador." Tim knew that helping out the Government would appeal to her vanity.

"Ok, I'll bell him and you can call him in about half hour." She gave him her husband's number and hung up.

"Will he help?" asked Yosuf.

"He wouldn't dare not to after he speaks to Lisa. That leaves us with the problem of the heroin. I am not happy about handing it over to a pile of drug dealers."

"What are our options, we need their help?" Yosuf said.

"It bothers me. That's all."

"Us staying alive and stopping ISIS carrying out whatever we have here bothers me more."

Tim was forced to concede the point. They packed up their gear and vacated the room. They had paid cash in advance and having had baths and set up the laptop that had served its purpose, they called a taxi and headed for the railway station. The train would take them to Victoria station in central London in a few hours. From there, they could take the underground to their destination.

Chapter 17

On the top floor of Thames House, Elaine Wilkins was catching up with the daily intelligence reports. She pursed her lips and exhaled loudly. It was always the same at MI5, plentiful intelligence and too few staff to investigate fully. Things had improved gradually from the total shambles it had been after 9/11 when they had been caught totally unprepared. For years the Irish problems had occupied them and they were more or less up to the task, but the Islamic threat had been very different.

They had, over the years, built up a good network within the IRA. They were far easier to follow, for example: meeting in pubs and of course, ethnically white, as had been the majority of the staff at MI5. The attack had taken them by surprise with not enough staff and it being far more difficult to apply surveillance, even if the staff could have blended with the targets, which they couldn't. The Islamic factions would meet at home or in Mosques, where they could not be easily observed. At one point, MI5 were using the London Transport police to follow people, as well as the police and their own staff.

Elaine was in her mid-fifties and had held the post for two years. MI5 liked to pick women chiefs. She suspected that as the organisation was playing catch up, the appointment of women gave the appearance that it was forward looking and modern whereas it was, in fact, creaking at the seams. She was fastidious in her dress and grooming and her strength had always been applying attention to detail. She was wearing her Sunday best today, a nice Gary Webber suit and a plain white blouse. Her shoes and handbag matched. She had her regular meeting scheduled with the Home Secretary later, to whom she was responsible, unlike MI6 who reported to the Secretary of State for foreign Affairs.

She was preparing her brief for the meeting when there was a knock on her door. "Come in," she called, slightly irritated.

Jeff Stiles walked into the room, "Morning," he said cheerily. Stiles had been recruited from the Navy, he was now in his early forties. He was tall, with dark brown eyes and a full head of black hair, handsome by all standards, despite having a prominent nose.

"Yes, Good Morning."

"Ooh, somebody's not in the best of humour today."

"Sorry, but I have to be ready for the Home Secretary and there is a pile of crap to get through."

"Well I should like to add to the crap," Stiles said. "You know me, I cannot resist a good mystery or an oddity, so I have been following up a bit of Intel that came via GCHQ Cheltenham." Based on the outskirts of Cheltenham, CCHQ employed over five thousand staff. It coordinated information gathered from media, emails, telephone conversations and satellites and other communications from around the Globe.

"I can never resist a bit of information about our mates at Vauxhall," He was referring to MI6. "Well, for some reason, they have decided to take over the running of the investigation, by the police into heroin smuggling, involving the usual suspects from Turkey."

"Why are they bothered about that? Is there a direct link to terrorist funding in the UK? If there is, surely we would be on top of that? What's it to do with them anyway?"

"I asked myself the same questions and wondered if the buggers were involved in a bit of one-upmanship, hoping to get an easy collar at our expense? So I delved a little further. Now, then it gets interesting. The order was external and the decision doesn't seem to have come from the Secretary of state but some junior Minister."

"COBRA initiative?" suggested Elaine. COBRA was the security committee chaired by the Prime Minister to deal with any significant threats and crises facing the Country.

"Again it does not appear so. That leaves us with what appears a direct intervention by a junior minister called, Terrance Mailer, into our territory. In other words, the investigation into the drug smuggling has been, effectively, side-lined."

"Now you have my interest. That is very curious indeed. Why would anybody want to stop an investigation into something nobody was interested in the first place, apart from a few Bobbies." She paused, "You didn't just leave it did you? You did some more digging. I know you, you had to pick away at it and now you want me to spend part of our meagre budget to poke around further? Am I right?"

He smiled, "You are the boss for a good reason. Of course I dug a bit more."

"And?"

"And … I searched around any related bits and pieces using our algorithms looking for links. It would appear that a Turkish translator was killed in Menton, near Monaco, and his wife and her brothers seem to have disappeared, or were made to disappear by Turkish Intelligence. A Drug dealer linked to the London drug cartel was blown up in Paris, the forensic of the bomb's construction suggesting an ISIS maker who the French have been trying to track down for a long while. Then I looked for a link and guess what turned up? Don't guess, I'll tell you," he smiled.

"Mehmet Yildirim, the Mr. fix-it for the Turks, Deputy Head of

Intelligence." He waited or her reaction.

She sat quietly and contemplated the facts. "What was this dead Turk doing in Menton?"

"He was not in Menton, he was with the Turkish delegation in Monte Carlo who had organised a beano for the Paris office. Now that has its own area of interest. Our friend Mehmet and his old school buddy, Jason Delonge, were part of the party. Curiously, not only did the Turks manage to get one of their staff murdered, they seem to have misplaced another, called Yosuf, a low level intelligence gatherer and head of their translation service. It seems that, not only have the Turks been careless in misplacing staff, we seem to have one of ours go missing as well, an Anthony Burr,"

"One of ours?"

"Sort of, he his paid for out of our budget to sift information and prepare situation briefings locally for the Ambassador." he said.

"Gives us legitimacy to investigate then?"

He laughed. "Why not, we always set up a full scale counter espionage operation when an employee doesn't make work on a Monday morning, don't we?"

"Funny ha, ha! Ok, what do you want? You have me intrigued. Do you know where the Turks run their drug operation from?"

"Wood Green, North London," he replied.

"There's a surprise, daft question really."

"I want a couple of bodies to put their headquarters under surveillance?" he said.

She thought for moment. Money was tight. "Go on then, I am curious to get to the bottom of it, but keep it cheap and cheerful."

Chapter 18

The train journey from Eastbourne to London had been uneventful, it had taken Tim and Yosuf about five minutes to walk from Victoria station to the Premier Inn where they had booked into a room. Lisa had been true to her word and Tim had a lunch appointment with her current husband John.

"Will you be alright on your own?"

"Fine," replied Yosuf.

"I saw a print and copy shop as we walked here. I shall print the contents of the memory stick to show to Mr Midas and leave the stick with you."

"And I, my friend, shall sample the delights of a burger and chips while you wine and dine in the finest eateries the City has to offer."

Tim took the Tube to Bank station, walked down Cornhill and turned into Ball Court. It was like stepping back into the eighteenth century. The courtyard was crowded with office workers on their lunch break. The eatery dated back to 1757 and it still retained the Dickensian feel. Tim had met John on a couple of occasions over the years and spotted him at the bar as he walked in.

"Ordered you a pint if that's ok?" John greeted him. He was slightly taller than Tim and immaculately turned out. If Tim were honest with himself, he would have admitted to being slightly envious of him. He had a natural charm and charisma that made people notice him. He supposed the difference was self-confidence.

When he walked in a room where he was unknown to the other guests, he would quietly move to the side of the room. John would confidently walk to the centre of the room, thrust out his hand and announce his name. The outcome was obvious. Even if he was unimportant and unknown to everyone, the fact that he expected to be greeted and exuded confidence, usually resulted in the most senior person there coming forward and shaking his hand. Being greeted by the head guy would in an instant confer his importance and status to those present.

"Fine," said Tim, even though he would have preferred a soft drink.

"Traditional ale, you can't beat it," said John.

"Perfect," Tim lied, as he took a swig of the bitter, tepid and warm beer.

"They have a table for us and it should be ready soon." The bar was packed and the clientele had spilled outside where they continued to drink and smoke. "So how are you?"

"Fit and well and you?"

"As a fiddle, but I am looking forward to getting out on the old yacht you know. We've had her sailed out to the Caribbean and Lisa and I are planning a quick trip round the Islands. Do you have a boat?"

John knew full well that he did not have a yacht and it was just his way of letting Tim know their relative positions in social standing. "No I don't."

"You should get one. Jolly good fun."

Luckily, John was interrupted by a middle aged woman in an apron. "There are a couple of spaces now, darling" she said. They followed her downstairs and were shown to two seats on opposite sides of a table that was attached to a wall at one end. Four diners were already in place, two on each side sat on the bench. A tall brass bowler hat stand divided the back to back benches. The age of bowler hats had long gone, but their use was now extended as a place to park laptops and briefcases.

"Now, what can I get you boys?"

"You know me Mary, the usual rump steak" said John.

"And you ducks?"

In the absence of being given a menu, Tim replied that he would have the same.

"Would you like a sausage with that?" asked Mary.

"Of course and a bottle of the house red," said John. She looked at Tim who nodded.

"Stylish carrier bag you have there. Does it contain what you want me to have a butchers at?"

"I should be very grateful if you would." He passed him the Copy Shop bag and its contents.

The wine turned up with two glasses that Tim poured as John read. John studied the documents for a while and flicked page after page. "Ok! Got it," he said.

"Well?"

"Well, I have not seen these for a while. They were a feature of the nineteen eighties. I need to give you a bit of background on the London insurance market if you are to make sense of it"

"Go ahead," said Tim.

"Well, around the time this place was established, coffee was a big thing. The merchants would meet up in coffee shops and do business. One of the most popular was one ran by a chap called Lloyd, who gave his name to the World's first insurance market. The big steel building up the road, designed by Richard Rogers, is where they live today and is now called Lloyds of London." He took a sip of claret.

"These merchants decided to spread the risk of their ships and trade. If a ship sank a merchant would have the total loss of the ship and its cargo. So they decided to share the risk between themselves and marine insurance was born." The steak turned up.

"The market evolved so that wealthy individuals, with no direct interest in the actual vessels or cargo, would participate in the risk of a voyage by receiving a premium in return for insuring the loss. As trade grew into the modern era, the cargos and ships become bigger and more valuable and even the wealthiest people became unable to withstand the losses on their own, so they started to lay off their risk. Re-insurance was born."

"Good sausage?"

"Very good," said Tim "Re-insurance?"

"It is like a bookie who lays off a bet with other bookies. Say you go into a bookies and place a hundred thousand pounds on a one hundred to one horse to win, he would lay that bet off with other bookies, So, perhaps, he would only be liable, if you won, for five percent of it and the rest of the bookies would stump up the balance. It is a way of sharing risk."

"What these papers relate to are what is referred to as 'Tonners.' Using the bookie analogy; a bookie could receive hundreds of laid off bets in a day from other bookies. In effect he would receive a share of the stake money from dozens of other bookies. So he could, theoretically, claim that he had a stake in the outcome of every win or loss in every race."

"I am not clear," said Tim.

"Underwriters, like the bookies, take re-insurance premiums from hundreds of other insurers so, one way or another, when a ship flounders they will, inevitably, have a smaller or larger share of the loss somewhere along the line."

"Tonners?" said Tim.

"A gamble really, the logic for it was: An insurer, through the re-insurance contracts he had written, has an interest in every ship in the World and when it sank he, theoretically, would have to pay out, so he could re-insurer that notional risk. The way the gamble worked was that one insurer would pay a premium, a bet really, saying that if a ship over a certain weight sank in a given period, he would receive ten or twenty times his premium, or bet from the other insurer. If nothing over that weight sank, he lost his premium."

"These papers show bets being placed into the insurance markets for the biggest ships in the World. The bets are big and the pay-outs would be massive," said John.

"How big?"

"A billion perhaps, or more, hard to say off the top of my head, but the likelihood of any ship of this size sinking is infinitesimal. I would say that the insurance companies who paid the premiums, or placed the bets if you like, have wasted their money."

"How come, surely ships sink all the time," said Tim.

"True, but these would be the size of super massive oil tankers and they don't sink very often. They are the biggest and the best."

"Stewed cheese?" interrupted Mary.

"Of course, what else?" answered John for both of them.

Tim considered the information, "Who benefits from this if one of these tankers sinks?"

"The insurance companies listed here," he looked at the list in front of them, "Mostly the arseholes of Alaska."

"What, the arseholes of Alaska?"

John smiled. "It a phrase we use for second rate insurers who are undercapitalised, poor security and usually located in some dodgy country. The ones on the list taking out these Tonners are mostly Middle Eastern and North African."

"Terrorist linked?" said Tim.

"Who knows, but at a guess they are used to launder money and move it around the World."

"Tell me if I have this right. If a super-sized oil tanker sinks, then these guys stand to receive millions from these so called insurances?"

"In a nutshell, yes."

"What do those columns of letters and numbers mean?" said Tim, pointing to the last sheet of paper.

"I am afraid I can't help you with that bit," he said.

"Did you enjoy your food, love?" asked Mary.

Tim had to admit that he had.

Chapter 19

Tim and Yosuf were on their drug run. They had left the hotel and boarded the tube at Victoria and after changing to the Piccadilly line at Finsbury Park, got off the train at Wood Green. It was beginning to get dark as they walked down the High Street past Toys R Us and turned down the road leading to "Spicy Chicken and kebab".

It was still quite early in the kebab world and the shop was empty. From eleven o'clock at night the place would be full of drunken teenagers in need of a greasy doner kebab before bed. They entered the shop. The smell of the slow cooking lamb on the rotating spite and the skewers of meat on the grill did have a delicious aroma and tempted them, despite the fact they had both eaten.

A Turkish worker in a red t shit, with the takeaway's logo and name on it, wearing a white folded hat, again displaying the logo, approached them at the counter. The takeaway, decorated in mostly red and yellow, had a glass entrance door, a few tables which you walked past in order to approach the counter that ran the width of the back of the shop.

"What can I get you?" asked the server.

Yosuf said the phrase, a password and glances were exchanged between the employees. The end of the counter was lifted and they were shown past the kitchen to what looked like the cold store. It was, in fact, a heavily reinforced door and required the employee to speak into an entry phone system to gain access for them.

Distributing heroin was a very hazardous occupation, you needed to be very well organised and security conscious. The doors in this kebab shop would have been the envy of many a bank.

Gang rivalry in London for drug distribution was intense and shootings and murders for turf were not uncommon. Wood Green was right in the heart of it with Tottenham and Finsbury Park a spit away. The area was divvied up between the various gangs, but conflict was inevitable. The Turks had a fierce reputation for extreme violence, gunfights were not uncommon. Things had recently quietened after the shooting of a police woman that had enraged public opinion. In truth, the drug dealers were careful not to harm the police or ordinary citizens, but matters had in this instance got out of hand when some Poles had tried to establish themselves.

The door swung back for them and a gang member showed them up a flight of stairs into what was, effectively, a café with tables and chairs. Coffee was on the brew with gang members playing the inevitable backgammon.

"Hello and welcome," said a middle aged, slightly overweight man. "my name is Jimmy and these are John and Mick. Not their real names of course." All three were Turkish. John and Mick looked formidable and were clearly not known for their sensitivity. "Is that for me?" he said looking at the cases.

He pointed at the two cases Tim and Yosuf were carrying. They had left their clothes and other belongings at the hotel and split the heroin between them. They passed the suitcases over to John and Mick, who in turn passed them over to two men who stopped playing back gammon and immediately left with them.

"Sit down," said Jimmy. They sat and were offered the mandatory sweet, thick and ground filled cup of Turkish coffee.

After a pause Jimmy spoke." A disturbing fact has come to light and I wonder if you may have anything to add. Your friend and my friend and colleague Osman has been killed. Were you aware of this fact?"

He studied their faces intently. They were clearly surprised and this seemed to re-assure him. "How?" asked Yosuf.

"In a very unusual fashion for our line of work, he was killed by a bomb. We do not like to use bombs, they may kill a rival, but they also may kill innocent bystanders and that is not good, it really draws attention to us and is very bad for business."

Tim was feeling very uneasy in the presence of this rather jolly rotund man, who casually discussed killing people so matter of factly. He realised that he was weighing up Tim's and Yosuf's involvement and deciding if the best course of action would be to have them disposed of and so overt any further danger to him.

Tim was regretting their decision to deliver the drugs at all. Yosuf had persuaded him to do so, based on the logic that adding the drug ring to the list, already containing Mehmet and ISIS, of people trying to hunt them down and kill them would not be a good idea.

"He was my friend, we grew up together, I am greatly saddened. I fear we may be partly to blame. We are being hunted and he helped us by getting us out of France, in return we have kept our part of the bargain and made the delivery safely to you," said Yosuf.

Jimmy studied him and considered. "I believe you. Had you been involved you would hardly walk in here. In any event, it may have nothing to do with you. Osman has had to deal with some very dangerous people to ensure the supply of our product. These people are driven by idealism and not profit. The bombing suggests ISIS and a dispute over the payment or such and after all you are dodging Turkish security, as are we all."

At that moment Jimmy's mobile rang three times then went silent. It rang again four times. "You may go now, my men have safely delivered the product to be cut and packaged." He spoke on the phone and turned to address them again." There is a car and driver out front, Mick and John will see you safely to the car. The driver will take you where you want to go. Safe journey," Jimmy said.

They exchanged handshakes and followed Mick and John down the stairs and out of the shop. It was now dark as the three of them left the shop and began the walk towards the car.

The next few minutes turned into a blur. Three men stepped forward, the ISIS trio, and just opened fire on them. Yosuf pushed Tim to the ground and simultaneously pulled his gun. Both Mick and John went for their guns. John fell to the ground, blood pumping from the gunshot wound in his neck. He shook violently as a fit engulfed him and blood spurted from his nose and mouth. He died chocking, gargling his own blood.

Yosuf lying on the ground, firing wildly in the direction of their assailants. Mick had his gun out and fired as he turned his back and started to run back to the shop. There was a burst of gunfire, his back became a mass of shredded clothing and flesh as he slowly slumped forward onto his knees screaming in agony.

Yosuf fired again. Tim finally moved and pulled his gun. A bullet skipped in front of where they lay and Yosuf let out a yell of pain as a fragment hit his arm. Tim raised his gun as the three ISIS assassins ran towards them. He fired the recoil, sending his arm jolting back and the bullet flying harmlessly off into the sky.

It seemed that all was lost and the assailants would soon have him and Yosuf. They were running towards them, closely followed by a black, Ford Transit van. They would soon be prisoners of these fanatics.

Tim fired again and as if by magic, one of them, the largest fell, his head exploding into a mess of brain and blood. The other two dropped to their knees and crouching, began shooting past Tim and Yosuf. Bullets were streaming past. The driver of the black van rolled down the window and began firing.

The doors to the kebab shop flew open and Jimmy and his men ran out onto the street firing in all directions, assuming they were being attacked by a rival drug gang.

Mehmet was running towards them with three operatives from the Turkish security firing at the terrorists. They were the better armed with Uzi 9mm machine pistols spraying short bursts. Tim grabbed Yosuf and made to run to the waiting car, but as they approached it drove off. One of Mehmet's soldiers sprayed it with bullets, the car veered across the road, wheels squealing and continued to accelerate and crashed into the Transit. The mix of bullets, twisted and smashed fuel tanks caused the vehicles to explode with a deafening roar of heat and flying shrapnel. The windows of the kebab shop were blown out, Jimmy and his men were showered in glass and flame.

The last ISIS soldier died in the onslaught, Jimmy and his men were screaming from their injuries. Mehmet's men fired a short burst in their direction then there was silence

Mehmet advanced on Tim and Yosuf as they staggered to their feet and began to run down street. They continued running. There was another burst of gun fire and Tim watched in horror as Yosuf staggered a few paces and fell forward. His face held a look of surprise as life faded from him. Tim had no time to stop and in shock, half expecting death to catch him as well, ran for his life.

Suddenly silence and then a voice "Stop this now MI5."

Mehmet stopped in his tracks. He and his men lowered their guns. He could probably kill drug dealers and terrorists on the streets of London with only a stiff protest at Government level, but he knew he could not kill a member of the British Security without very bad consequences for him and Turkey.

"You lot fuck off," Jeff Stiles said waving Mehmet back. Tim just kept running.

Chapter 20

The small village in Northern Iraq where Dr Jaffer worked was in the main quiet and mostly peaceful. He had two children Mem, Akram and a wife Telenaz. The rule of Saddam Hussein and the Ba'th party was, of course, a restrictive factor in all their lives. Dr Jaffer was part of the Muslim minority in this part of the country, being a Sunni Muslim.

The majority of the World's Muslims, some one and a half billion people, are Sunni. The word Sunni is derived from "Ahl al-sunnah," people of tradition and they based their religion on what the Prophet Muhammad practiced, preached or condemned. The Shia Muslims derived their name from "Shiat Ali" the party of all. They claim that Ali, the leader of the Muslims following the death of the Prophet Muhammad, in 632 AD, was his Prophet's rightful successor. The majority of the Muslims in Iraq are Shia Muslims.

Mem and his brother Akram, who was just a toddler, were not aware of these factors of course. They went to school, .played with friends and applied themselves to their studies to the extent that children do. From an early age, their Father would lecture them on the importance of education. He was proud of his two sons and hoped that one day they would follow him into medicine.

Mem would come home from school and find the downstairs of their house filled with patients from the village. His Mother had met his Father at the hospital when he was a junior doctor and where she was a nurse. When he qualified they had moved back to the village where her parents and family lived and set up the practice. Mem's aunties, uncles and cousins all lived within half a mile, all Sunnis in a predominantly Shia area.

Mem's closest friend was Gabir, they used to do everything together. As he entered his Father's waiting room, he saw Gabir's Father sitting in the waiting area. He called Mem over and reaching in his pocket, handed him a sweet. "Were you and Gabir well behaved at school today?" He withheld the sweet teasing him.

"Of course," he replied cheekily, grabbing the sweet.

"Come to our house tomorrow, we are having a BBQ," he called as Mem disappeared upstairs.

"Are you eating a sweet," asked his Mother sternly. "You will not eat your meal and you will have no teeth," she cautioned.

Mem remembered the family evening meals together, sat around with the delicious treats his Mother would cook up, then television, before homework and bed. His Father was very strict about the homework. Of course, as he became older he would try and wriggle out of the homework part and extend the television part but on the whole, he had worked hard and was doing well at school.

Gabir's home was a far more modest affair than Mem's house, a single story building in the Shia part of town. There was a plot of land to the side of the house. It was more a dry patch of scrub and gravel where the open fire was spitting when Mem arrived for the BBQ. The neighbourhood as a whole was run down and the houses unkempt and Gabir's house was no exception.

"Welcome," shouted Gabir, as they approached. "We have lots of food." Iraq had lots of shortages from milk to medicines and the simple basics like washing up liquid. The US sanctions led the way in imposing restrictions on Saddam Hussein's regime. After the attack on the Twin Trade Towers in New York, the Americans seemed to be looking to take revenge and Iraq fell into the firing line. Although the attacks had been mounted by Al–Qaeda and

Saddam Hussein's ruling Ba'th party had vigorously opposed them, this did not seem to matter to the Americans or the British. The American president, George Bush and the British Prime Minister, Tony Blair were committed to the toppling of Saddam Hussein's regime.

"It smells so good," said Mem and they rushed over to the BBQ. Akram held onto his hand, struggling to keep up.

Things changed suddenly. No one knew at first how much life would change, but they all were hopeful for things to get better. The news was filled with propaganda extolling how the great Iraqi army would obliterate the imperialist, infidel invaders and remove them from the face of the planet. It was to be in Saddam's words "The Mother of all Battles." It did not quite turn out that way.

The war started with an air strike on the Presidential Palace on the twentieth of March and despite the rhetoric, the War was over within months. Saddam Hussein was gone and the coalition forces had taken control. Mem remembered his Father and Mother being so happy when Saddam Hussein had been toppled. They had danced in the streets. They had embraced their friends and neighbours.

It had not remained that way. Friends and neighbours soon turned on each other. There were no police, no military and no law and order. Militia roamed the streets and the Country became divided into differing Muslim factions. Looting, killing and bombings in the street and markets became the norm.

Mem's Father tried to carry on doing what he knew best, being a doctor. Helping and treating the sick, but the Shia Muslims were becoming more empowered and resentment and religious fever took over. The sectarian violence spread from city to town and from town to village. Then one night it reached into Mem's home. Mem, Akram and his Mother cowered upstairs as his Father was dragged by the mob from their home. Mem could not bear it and broke free from his Mother's arms and ran downstairs.

He saw his Father pushed along the street by the mob to join the men and older boys already gathered in a fearful, beaten and bloodied mass. The mob chanted, beat and spat at them as they herded them to the edge of the village.

He hid in the darkness as the group was lined up. He could clearly see his Fathers face, his uncle, grandfather his entire extended family outlined in the moonlight. He could hardly believe it as Gabir's Father stepped forward from the crowd holding a gun. He was joined by others. He spat at Dr Jaffer, raised his gun and shot him in the face. He remained standing for a brief moment, then to a cheer from the mob, his knees buckled and he sank slowly to the ground. Mem watched frozen as the rest of his extended family suffered the same fate. Mem would never forget the look of satisfaction on Gabir's Fathers face as he watched the doctor die.

"Father is dead," he said simply with grief and dignity to his Mother, "We have to leave this place. They will not let us live if we stay." He remembered gathering together some clothes and a blanket. He picked up the book his Father had given him. Schooling had stopped months before. It was far too dangerous to attend the Mosque. It just made them too easy to be identified by the vigilante groups, who wanted to dispose of them. His Father had tried to keep up his education and his study of the Koran. Dr Jaffer had given Mem the book only days before on history and civilisation "Gods of Ancient Egypt." He put it in his rucksack. It was all he had left of his Father.

They had set out with their meagre possessions, his Mother carrying what she could with Akram tied in a shawl across her chest. They had been set upon before they left the village and anything of value plundered from them. Telenaz had wept as they took her jewellery, the last connection she had to her husband.

They were surrounded by the mob as they reached the edge of

their village. They began to shout and abuse her physically. Like frenzied dogs the pack mentality was in control. The mob began to tear at her clothes and grabbing at her exposed naked breasts. Mem tried to fight them, but was held firmly by two of the men. Gabir's Father stepped forward and fired his gun into the air. Silence feel and they all looked at him. "Let them go," he said. She was spared rape but that was all. Every ounce of dignity had been taken from her. Battered, bruised and with nothing, they escaped.

Mem remembered days of walking and hunger. At times so tired, so hungry all that could be done was to put one foot in front of the other. There was some kindness along the way, but mostly indifference and cruelty. The whole country was broken, no government, no police or administration. It was a free for all where the only way to survive was to arm yourself and band together. The Americans and the British, having disbanded the mechanism of government left by Saddam, had to rely on the various militia factions to keep some form of order.

The trek to the border took weeks, Day after day of walking, hiding, hunger and more hunger and fatigue, after three months they reached Turkey. The boarder had proved very easy to cross and still proves the same today with ISIS entering more or less when they wanted. Of course, ISIS were not a reality then, but Iran was causing as much mayhem as they could in Iraq, by supplying weapons and funds to the various factions, in a bid to humiliate the Americans. From the cauldron of fragmented groups across the region, ISIS would coalesce into a force to threaten all before it, with its goal of reviving the Caliphate.

Mem would take the book out and read it every day. It became a symbol of his Father's love and a trigger for the memory of his life before this now permanent state of wondering and hunger. He read it. He memorised it. He saw the pictures of the Ancient Egyptian gods. He wished they existed and would punish those that had destroyed his entire family. He looked at the book and imagined them being called by Annubis, the jackal headed god, to be judged by Thoth, with the head of Ibis, who would then weigh their souls against a feather. Those that failed and judged evil would be fed to Sobek, the crocodile god. He wanted so badly that those guilty of so many crimes against his family would be ripped to pieces and fed to the crocodiles.

When they eventually reached Turkey, there was no sympathy or respite, just more discrimination and violence, hunger and isolation. He remembered the camps where rape, theft and murder were an everyday occurrence. His Mother struggled and eventually worn down by grief and fatigue just gave up. She just stopped living. He watched her die. Mem tried the best he could to survive, stealing and scavenging and bringing in what money and food he could to keep himself and Akram alive. But he was only fourteen and he could not do it on his own. The Red Crescent visited the camps and he and Akram were rescued and taken to a home for orphans.

"Mem," he remembered his Mother's dying words as he stood before her clutching his brother's tiny hand. She was shaking and tears ran down her face. "You must be strong for you are now a man." He was far from a man, but for a moment he felt strength that soon faded into despair

The children's home was a dingy, filthy building with little food, no education and bug ridden mattresses to sleep on. Mem would be awakened at six and the local farmer would pull up in the truck. "Come on, get a move on you lazy trash." The farmer shouted as the boys climbed up on to the back of the flatbed. The mornings were cold and their breath could be seen in the frosty air. They sat exposed on the back of the truck, the wind chilling them further.

With numb hands and chattering teeth and hunger in their belly, they were set to work. The farmer treated the boys as animals. "Faster," he would shout. Always faster, he was indifferent to their pain. He had paid the home for labour and he was going to get his money's worth. The food was meagre and infrequent, but the farmer made sure they just got enough to keep them working. The people in charge of the home not only benefited from the direct payment for the child labour, but they could also pocket the savings they made from not feeding the boys.

Sometimes a limousine would drive up from Istanbul and collect the children for, so called, parties in the houses of the rich. Mem, being older, was less popular than the younger boys, but he had been to the parties and forced to perform sexual acts and be sodomised. He hated them all and wished Annubis would descend and gather them up. He didn't.

The torment was worse when they took Akram. Small with big oval eyes and soft olive skin he was a favourite, he was often taken in the limo. Mem would try and comfort him as he lay on a dirty mattress sobbing and bleeding from his anus, his small body covered in bruises and lips swollen. He just would huddle in a ball, holding his stomach and clinging to Mem. Mem's hatred grew day by day.

Then one day, the limo came and took Akram, but this time it did not bring him back. The next day, Mem was frantic. He tried asking the lout in charge where his brother was, but he was beaten for his pains and ignored. Akram never came back.

Mem grew and became strong and he started killing when he was seventeen. First the sweaty pig who ran the home and then each and every one who had used and abused him and his brother. As the years passed, he became very good at killing and people paid him well for his talent. He had one last one person he needed to kill for his brother. He did not know his name, but he would never forget his face, the man who came to collect him in the big shinny car and never brought him back.

Annubis, as he was now known to those who employed his services, sat in an airless room listening to the ISIS representative.

"This is your target," he said and passed an envelope across the floor.

"Why are you employing me? Why not use your own people?" said Annubis, as he picked up the envelope.

"You do not need to know, but we specifically want this individual dead. We do not have the expertise for this, bombings and military action yes, but targeted assassination is not what we have the training for. This man is heavily protected at all times. He just killed someone close to me." Nizar looked down at the picture of his brother, killed., in Wood Green in London two days ago. Nizar and his brother had both left England together and went Syria to train. Nizar had remained and had risen through the ranks of ISIS. His brother had returned to Turkey and coordinated ISIS activities in the West.

Annubis left the room, counted the money and looked at the photograph. Mehmet looked back at him. His heart raced with elation. At last he had found him, the man in the limo, now vengeance for his brother was his to take.

Chapter 21

The passengers streamed out of Westminster Station into the early morning rain. Elaine Wilkins joined the mass of bodies squeezing into lines to navigate the ticket barriers. She was not looking forward to her day at work, a day that had actually begun at two o'clock that morning with frantic phone calls from Government officials and heads of departments.

As she jostled her way out of the exit she glanced up at Big Ben and decided she had time for a coffee. She stopped at the newspaper seller and picked up a copy of a poplar tabloid before entering Starbucks and ordering a double espresso. She needed something strong and black to get her started this morning. Struggling to carry her oversized briefcase, paper and coffee she managed to elbow herself onto a raised seat facing the window. The workers scurried past, umbrellas drawn all trying to get to work on time. She, on the other hand, really felt the opposite. She really didn't feel like facing the shit storm that would be her day.

At that precise moment, she felt the need for a cigarette and pondered if it had been worth the effort of quitting when it was quite obvious that, with a few more days like this, she would die of a stress induced heart attack. She rummaged in her coat pocket and found her reading glasses and now spectacled, she turned her attention to the newspaper. She did not need to read long. There on the front page was all that she needed to know.

"Drug battle on streets of Capital," it read. She read on," Eight dead in shoot out on streets of London." It got worse, comparing

London to Chicago in the nineteen thirties and pointing the finger at the police and the security agencies.

She got up, binned the paper and trudged reluctantly along Millbank to Thames House and MI5's headquarters. The walk was longer than she remembered. She had a car at her disposal and was usually collected from home and chauffeured to her office. She had today fancied a change and felt the need to connect with reality and feel what it was like to travel on the overcrowded London transport system. She was seriously beginning to regret that decision as her feet started to throb in her expensive high heeled shoes. She loved her shoes and she indulged herself frequently in that passion. Although the shoes looked fabulous they did fail in one major aspect, that of being a shoe. They were completely unsuitable for walking in. She gave up after a hundred yards, flagged a black cab and rode the rest of the way.

The door opened and Jeff Stiles walked into her office. "Good Morning."

"Don't be so fucking cheerful," Elaine said by way of a greeting. "What happened?"

Jeff sat down and recounted the sorry tale. He had organised the surveillance on the kebab shop in Wood Green the previous night in the hope of making contact with Tim and Yosuf, He had two men sat in a car down the street watching the shop. The plan was simple. If they were on foot they would follow them on foot or alternatively in the car, find out where they were and tell Stiles, who in turn would have a chat with them and find out what was going on. Sadly things had not turned out as planned.

Jeff had got into the car, "Anything?"

The driver responded," Nothing as yet, a few people buying kebabs and a few dodgy types going in and staying in."

The passenger continued eating a burger and sucked a large drink in a cup through a straw. "Hold that," he shoved the burger and drink over his shoulder towards Jeff, who was sat on the back seat. For a brief moment he looked like he would be wearing a burger and showering in cola, but he managed to get control of the meal avoiding the consequences. He placed the half-finished burger onto the seat next to him.

He raised his binoculars to his eyes and then passed them to Jeff. "That's them, Sir."

Jeff could clearly see the two characters walking down the street hauling a suitcase each. He hastily grabbed the file from the passenger seat and in the process knocked the cola over the back seat and himself. He compared the photos to the two men as they came closer. "Yes, that is definitely them." They entered the takeaway and disappeared from view, "Have you got some serviettes?" he threw the meal out of the car window and began to mop his leg and the car seat.

While they waited for them to re-emerge, Jeff had ample time to moan about his sticky wet leg. The driver said, "Do you see that black van?"

"What about it?"

"Wasn't it parked here when we arrived?"

"So"

"Doesn't it strike you as odd that it hasn't picked up a parking ticket? We had to have a quiet word with the warden or we would be festooned in them by now. So why isn't that van plastered with them?"

"Give me the bins, I think I can read the number plate from here." said Jeff. He focussed the lenses and managed to get half the plate in view. "Fuck CD." Corps Diplomatic, an embassy car, it had diplomatic immunity. Most governments voluntarily complied with local laws and paid fines but some didn't and exercised their right not to pay. "Run the plate." He managed to figure out the rest of the registration.

"Turkish Embassy," was the reply.

"Shit," said Jeff, but before he could react, a Mercedes pulled up outside the takeaway and the door opened as two men accompanying Tim and Yosuf left the shop. Then three further men appeared from nowhere and began shooting at the group leaving the takeaway. The doors to the black Transit had opened and suddenly a shit storm of gunfire was in full progress. More armed individuals poured from the shop adding to the hail of gunfire and confusion.

"Fuck me," said the driver.

"Fuck me, indeed," added Jeff. The Turkish Secret Service was the clear winner and Jeff decided to get out of the car and break up the party.

What happened after?" asked Elaine impatiently.

"Mehmet called a halt not wishing to set back Turkish diplomatic relations with the UK a hundred years and matters seemed more or less under control."

"You call that under control? The street littered with dead Turks. You have a very strange idea of the meaning of under control."

Jeff ignored his boss's sarcasm and continued. "As I said, matters were calming down and then Anthony decided to leg it. I ordered the lads to give chase."

"So where is our Mr Burr?" asked Elaine.

"The next thing we know, armed response police appear from every direction waving machine guns and they have a bloody helicopter overhead and the lot of us are bundled up and carted off to the nick." He paused, "Thanks for getting us out, by the way"

"I repeat, where is Anthony Burr, now?"

"I am sorry, we just do not know."

"Well bloody well find him and bring him here" she said. "At least the press have bought the drug war angle and we can forget about the Turks as they are on their way back to Ankara, after the usual expelling of diplomats malarkey," she continued.

"Find Burr and try not to start a war, there's a good boy. I shall now try and sort this out with my Minister," she looked at her watch. "Bugger, I am late," she gathered up her bag, stood up and felt her feet pinch in her shoes.

"One final thing," she called as Jeff left her office. "Take my advice. Make sure you wear sensible shoes."

Chapter 22

The sun flooded in through the crack in the curtains and a shaft of light entered the hotel room. Little dust particles created ever moving patterns. They seemed to tumble and rise, changing colour as they rotated, endlessly trapped in their prison of brightness in an otherwise darkened room.

Tim just stared at the light. He was bewildered. Up to this point he had felt a little detached from events. Thinking back after finding Berat's body in that tiny room in Menton, events had taken control of him. Yosuf had guided him through. Shocked and in shock, he had more or less been a bystander, but with the violent death of his friend on the streets of North London the previous night, it was no longer possible to just stay on for the ride. He realised he was now the focus of something very big and very dangerous.

The night had been long and sleepless. A continuous rerun of the events replayed in his mind in ever increasing detail. Tiny details popped into his head, the sound of a gun, a muzzle flash, an expression on a face, a detail on a face such as a mark or scar. All ran round and round in his mind.

He just kept staring at the beam of light as it filtered into the room as if it contained some mystic secret. Then recurring was Yosuf, bloody, dying, lying beside him. He saw the look of pain, fear and resignation as the life passed from him. He felt hollowness in the pit of his stomach, a mix of fear and grief. He continued to stare at the light unmoving, grieving for hours.

He felt dreadfully alone and wanted to reach out to someone, feel reassured, feel safe and above all, feel hope. He was lost. He had relied on Yosuf to a great extent to do his planning and show the way forward. He had only known the man a few days, but the bond had formed and interdependency was part of that bond. They had become friends, trusting each other and relying one on the other. That was the past, Tim needed a future.

Tim finally roused himself to answer the call of nature. Even when you grieve, you still need to go to the toilet. He looked in the bathroom mirror. He looked like he felt, like a man who had been awake most of the night. He motivated himself and turning on the shower stepped under the stream of water. He let the warm water bathe his body and standing there tried to order the events of last evening. It was so fast, but from the first shot being fired, the rush of adrenaline had seemed to slow it all down so he could virtually re-run events in slow motion.

Who were the three men who appeared firing? They had to be ISIS. They had to be part of the group that had killed Berat and they had traced Yosuf and him all the way from France. It was now clear to Tim that they had shot at the drug dealers and not at Yosuf or him. They wanted them alive or at least they wanted the memory stick before they killed him.

He recognised the leader of the other group from the Yacht in Monte Carlo. That was Mehmet and he had had no compunction in killing Yosuf. Tim was pretty sure he would have only been kept alive long enough for them to get the memory stick. Of course, when the rest of the drug gang poured out of the Kebab Shop armed to the teeth with guns blazing it had turned into the gunfight at the OK Coral, just bullets and bodies everywhere. Then all had stopped, silence apart from that lone voice. Tim remembered getting up and running from the scene and as if he were invisible, had walked through the carnage, past all the various gunmen and through the police armed response team.

111

Unchallenged, he had just walked away up the road and boarded the underground train back to central London and his hotel.

He slowly dressed himself and sat on the bed. He got up and drew the curtains back and the beam of light, with its dancing hoard of dust, vanished. His eyes landed on Yosuf's bag. He felt sadness rush over him, but knew he had to sort things out. He opened the bag and spread the contents on the small writing desk before him.

There was money, lots of money in lots of different currencies. There were ID's, about twenty, all with Yosuf's photo on them. No use to Tim. He carried on examining the contents. There were some faded photos. A woman, a man, children and a young Yosuf smiling, his family thought Tim. A pile of credit cards fell from a big envelope. He examined the names, all different. There was a list of pin codes and security answers on a sheet of paper that matched the number on each card. These would be useful if they were useable. Tim needed to check the balances on them. The thing he did not want to do was present a credit card and have it declined as stolen or exceeding its credit limit.

Then there was the laptop. He switched it on and it came to life. It was pristine, no files, no sign of previous use. They had only used it to read the memory stick. The internet icon came up showing connections were available and the hotel name came up. Tim knew that they had been given the password when they had checked in and it was on a card somewhere on the desk. He began to pack the bundles of money and cards into his own bag and tidy up,

He knew clearly that Jason Delonge was not to be trusted. Yosuf had told all about Jason and the small boy with the oval eyes. As he thought of the child he had killed, his loathing for the man intensified. With such a horrendous crime, Tim also knew that Jason would not stop at anything to get himself off the hook.

His mind turned to the voice calling for calm last night. The voice was shouting "MI5". Tim could not be sure if Jason had enough influence to convince MI5 that he and Yosuf were, perhaps, traitors or terrorists. He could only be sure of one thing, that MI5 clearly had not been working with Mehmet and the Turkish Security Service. He further realised that they had not been shooting at anyone the previous evening and more to the point, they had not been trying to shoot Yosuf or him. He put that knowledge on the backburner for the moment.

Tim decided he had to eat and plan his next move. He locked the cases and put a do not disturb sign on the door. He worried that the amount of money and valuables in the room would tempt anyone into becoming a thief, but what could he do. He needed somewhere to keep everything, but that was easier said than done. Before the terror attacks you could just go into a railway station and leave your luggage in a locker, that option no longer existed for fear of a bomb being left.

Sitting in the dining room, he drank his coffee and ate the continental breakfast and gradually decided the course of his actions. He would ask his ex-Lisa, using one of the unregistered mobiles, if she would store some stuff for him, either at her office or at her flat in London. He would check the balances on the credit cards left by Yosuf. That would involve logging into the hotel internet service and using the codes on the list to check each one individually. Finally, he needed to decipher the last part of the information on the memory stick.

As he stood, he pondered the fact that a large number of suspect Insurance Companies, with possible links to ISIS, had placed huge bets on a very large ship sinking. If this happened, the terrorists would be billions of dollars to the good. He knew he needed help to unravel the memory stick, but he did not know who to ask. He had seen, the previous evening, that asking the wrong person would result in a swift bullet to his head and it was evident that neither ISIS nor the Turks had qualms about shooting people on the streets of the Capital.

Returning to his room, he sat down at the small desk and connected the laptop to the internet. He then, methodically, checked the balance on each card. He was astonished. There were over twenty cards, all with approximately ten thousand on each. Yosuf had planned this for a long time. Tim also realised that Yosuf had been a bit of a fraudster, helping himself to a large part of his department's operational budget. Of course, corruption was the norm in many of these countries and as everyone was in on it, fingers of blame were very unlikely to be pointed. Yosuf had merely set himself up a pension fund in the event he needed to take early retirement, before someone like Mehmet retired him permanently and prematurely.

He made a quick check of his emails before closing down the connection and phoning his wife. He only managed to get her voice mail. He decided to leave it and phone back a bit later. He felt better in himself in the fact that his was doing something. He turned his mind to the list of coded numbers from the memory card. He decided that he may get help from his University and decided that he would look up his old tutor, with whom he had kept in contact over the years and see if he would help him find someone in the mathematics department who could take a crack at deciphering it. A plan at least, he thought.

Chapter 23

The sky glowed red and orange and the temperature began to drop as night fell over the desert landscape. Annubis lit the little gas stove and emptied a tin of spaghetti into the small camping pan. It tasted like shit, but it was food. The Toyota Hilux had taken him miles deeper into Iraq, after he had left his meeting with ISIS.

He was going home. When he had seen the photo, of the scumbag who had used him and taken his young brother, he knew that this was the time to settle all matters. He had searched for years for Mehmet, but could not track him down. Of course, he had not known that their abuser was part of the Turkish Security Service and as such, would have been impossible to identify. So he had become a killer for hire, a hit man and assassin, but with just a single driving force, revenge. Then a gift, a divine gift it seemed from God, in a plain brown envelope just handed to him, the photograph of his nemeses. Just like that, a commission for him to be killed.

Annubis knew that he was to fulfil destiny. His Father, his uncles, his cousins, grandfathers, wives, children, nieces and nephews killed. Why? God's will? Because they believed in a different branch of Islam?

e sat in the moonlight looking at the distant village. He had covered the truck with brush so its outline was broken and merged into the background. The journey had been slow. The Country was still run by various militias and he had to avoid them as he made his way to this point. It was late and the village slept as he walked down the track to the place he had called home. It was a wreck of a place now, walls were down, holes were in the road, rubbish scattered around and buildings partly demolished, but still being lived in.

He looked at their old house, shabby, neglected with junk piled high in the garden that once his Mother had tended carefully and loved so much. Where they had sat as a family and shared their evening meal, where he had played with his brother and cousins. The walls of the building were bleached and the paint peeled and foliage grew on the neglected walls of the building.

Sadness ate into his soul as he waited in the moonlight. He felt emotional and a tear formed in his eye. This was the first feeling he had experienced since he had gone into himself on the loss of his brother. He was now sure what he should do. It was clear. Now was the time. He had weighed the souls of these people and they were heavier than a feather. Judgment was long overdue. He felt the pistol in his hand. It was unbalanced with the weight of the silencer.

The door was not locked and he entered his old home. His Father's waiting room had now been refurbished. The chairs that once lined the wall where the patients sat were gone as were the posters that gave medical advice on topics ranging from hand washing to teeth brushing. In his mind's eye he could see his Mother ushering the patients through and handing their files to his Father. He could see his Father stretching after a day of seeing the sick and walking up the stairs to spend the evening with his family.

Annubis walked slowly and silently up the same stairs. He could hear snoring and the rhythmic breathing of those sleeping in what was once his home. He stepped through the door of the first bedroom and looked down on the sleeping figure. The moonlight filtered in and he stood waiting for his eyes to adjust. He studied that figure. He knew him well, Gabir, his childhood friend. He remembered the sweets his Father had given him, the games they played and the BBQ in the garden. He placed the silencer to his head and pulled the trigger. The silencer restricted the sound of the discharge to a small cough. He watched as the small thin line of red spread into a large pool of blood. He reached into his pocket and withdrew a small white feather. He had weighed Gabir's soul against it and it was found to be heavier. He allowed the feather to float slowly down and watched it settle on the pool of blood. He watched as it turned slowly from white to red absorbing the blood and the guilt of the sinner in death.

In the next room lay Gabir's sister. She had been a baby when his Mother and he had fled for their lives, Innocent, he shot her anyway. He then moved to the next room and shot the other daughter, not even born when his Father died.

He lay next to his wife snoring. "Wake up," he said and turned the light on. They struggled from sleep, confused to be faced with him stood there, gun in hand. The shock and fear spread across their faces. "Say good bye to your wife," he shot her in the head. The skin, blood and brains sprayed over Gabir's Father. The grey and red blubbering mass hung from his face and across his chest. He was in a state of panic, gasping for breath and trembling like a jelly. Annubis remembered his gloating face as he had shot his Father.

"Stand up," he waived the gun at the blubbering wreck of a man lying in the bed. He struggled to his feet, trying to avoid the remains of his wife's brains. Annubis could see that he had pissed himself in fear. His Father had faced death like a man, standing defiantly keeping his bowels in check unlike the piece of shit that had murdered him.

"I should like to show you the cost of renting this house and the price you will pay for murdering my Father." He marched him to each of his children's rooms, showing him their bleeding dead bodies. He cried and pleaded for his life. Now he knew that the price was the death of all those that he loved. Annubis pulled the trigger and placed a feather on his corpse.

He then went to his uncles, aunties and grandparents houses. Twenty three further feathers were left before he drove away. He felt a sense of tranquillity and calm, almost of fulfilment as left his old village.

He knew that this was just the beginning. It was time for all matters to be settled and all bills to be paid. He would be in Turkey soon and Mehmet awaited him.

Chapter 24

Tim had heard nothing back from his ex-wife Lisa. He was left with the problem of the contents of Yosuf's bag. He knew walking around London, stuffed to the gills with cash and credit cards, was not a truly viable option. He needed somewhere to hide it. He emptied the contents onto the table to decide which items he should keep about his person and which items needed to deposited elsewhere.

He tipped the case upside down on the table and began to build piles. Cash in one, credit cards in another and fake ids in a third. The ids which had photos of Yosuf were clearly of no use to him and would have to be disposed of. He decided that he would find a bin to dump them in. He then noticed the memory stick. He must have missed this when he had previously rummaged through the contents.

He switched on the PC and inserted the stick. He found it was a video file and clicked on play. He knew instantly what he was seeing. There on the screen was Jason Delonge and the boy with the large oval eyes. He watched for as long as he could bear it and was nearly sick. Tim knew that, if nothing else came from this whole big mess he had become entangled in, Jason needed to be exposed for the piece of scum he was. Tim had not really felt hatred before, but now he hated two men with a vengeance, Mehmet and Jason.

He put the memory stick in his pocket where it joined the other he had been carrying for days. He still had the problem of deciphering the last part of the information. He had no luck in contacting his old University tutor who was away on a lecture tour.

He looked around the room for a place to hide the items piled in front of him. He looked for an air vent, grill or the like having seen the loot being stashed in such a location in every gangster film he had seen. Sadly, this hotel did not provide rooms with the option of storage air vents. He decided he would have to go to his ex-wife's office and ask her to look after the stuff. He had no other course of action open to him. He packed the case and left to walk to the tube station.

"We have a hit," said Jeff Stiles, as he entered Elaine Wilkins' office in MI5's headquarters at Thames House.

"Don't you ever knock?"

"Sorry, but I thought you would want to hear it immediately, something broke."

"I do have other things to do, you know," she said, "like explaining what happened in North London the other night to the Minister."

"Oh yeah! How did that go?" he said disinterestedly.

"I can see that you are really interested so I shall tell you."

"You know me. I can't be bothered with all the political stuff."

"It's a little thing called democracy and accountability," she said with a hint of irritation in her voice. "I explained the situation as best as we could understand it. To be honest, I sort of gave the impression that we had foiled a terrorist plot and broken up an ISIS cell."

"Well we did, sort of."

"No we did not. We actually stood by and watched a shoot-out between the Turks, drug dealers and some actual terrorists who supply the heroin trade in England. Not to mention the fact that we managed to lose Mr Burr, who casually wondered off while we managed to get ourselves arrested."

"As I said, we managed to foil a terrorist plot." Elaine couldn't help a smile at Jeff's remark.

"Ok," she said "what do you have?"

"GCHQ have located our Mr Anthony Burr. They got a hit on his email. He logged on and bingo. They are just tracing it through the ip address and should have a location within the hour."

"Has this information gone to MI6 as well?"

"We assume so."

"We need to find out what their involvement is," she said.

She picked up the phone and spoke. "Get me an appointment with M please." After James Bond every one referred to the head of MI6 as M. It was a standing joke that had stuck. The head's name was Bernard Waverly.

"What do you want us to do?" asked Jeff.

"As soon as you get a location, get there and bring him in."

The phone rang. "Ok I shall leave now."

"I am off to Vauxhall Cross," she said as she gathered up her papers. "Do not fuck this up. Just bring him in quietly," she said as her parting shot.

******

Tim's meeting with his wife had not been a pleasant affair, but after some argument, she had agreed to hold onto his bag and had locked it in her office. He had taken a taxi back from the City to the West End that had resulted in an ear pounding from the driver, who had strongly held opinions on any subject that could be named. Tim had listened to how the European Union was bad, the England football team was worse and that the state of the roads was appalling.

Tim was relieved as he left the cab at the hotel. He paid the fare and gave the obligatory tip and entered the foyer. He walked up the stairs to the first floor where his room was located and inserted his plastic card in the lock. Green light on, he opened the door and entered the room.

As he entered the room, he was instantly seized by two men and pulled inside. He thought of employing his years of martial arts training, but restrained himself as the man in the lighter grey suit shoved an id in his face, "Secret Intelligence Service," he said. "Please behave, we need to ask you a few questions."

They had been in the process of searching his room and one of them, who Tim categorised as the dark grey sort, continued to do so. While the light grey suit said, "we should like to take you along with us to answer a few questions." Tim knew it was not a request. The man then patted him down. "Anything I should know about?" Tim shook his head and he was ordered to empty his pockets.

Tim complied, but left the two memory sticks in the crease at the back of his trouser pocket and turned both his pockets inside out, It was an old trick magicians used to convince punters they had empty pockets while concealing a card or coin. As a lad, Tim had been interested in conjuring for a while, to impress his friends, He did not think for a minute such and old trick would work on professionals, but to his surprise, it did. They handed Tim back his wallet and bits and pieces which he put back in his pockets.

As one of them continued his search, Tim feared they would discover the Makarov. He had managed to hide it in the bathroom where he had found a small inspection panel in the tiling that housed a stop cock. It was attached with loosely held screws, Tim had opened it when he had been searching for a hiding place earlier. It was too small of course for the contents of the case, but just large enough to secrete the gun. His fears were unfounded.

"Let's go," said dark suit.

They got in the lift and Tim was lightly held by both men as they approached the foyer. They crossed the vestibule, the doors opened and they walked through onto the pavement.

"Stop right there," said Jeff Stiles, showing his MI5 credentials.

"The fuck we will," said light suit.

"Don't be stupid. This is our jurisdiction and Mr Burr is an MI5 employee. So get your hands off him." Jeff and his two colleagues had made their way over from Thames House as soon as they received Tim's location from GCHQ. They had checked with reception and knew that Tim had used his room key and was in the room. What they did not know was that Tim had two MI6 agents as company. They decided to wait until Tim left the building and bring him in quietly.

"How is he your employee, that's bollocks?"

We pay his wages, that's why. So hands off and fuck off," smiled Jeff.

"No way, we have our orders and we are taking him with us."

"Who gave you these orders," Elaine Wilkins appeared. The two MI6 suits recognised the head of MI5. She had just left Vauxhall Cross following her meeting with Waverly and received Jeff's message saying he had a location for Tim. She had ordered her driver to bring her to the hotel where the scene was playing out,

"Ma'am, we do have orders," dark suit said, rather less assertively.

"I am not deaf young man. I heard you the first time. Take your hands off Mr Burr and tell me who issued the orders."

"With all respect, I cannot do that."

Elaine pulled out her phone and dialled. A few words were exchanged and she passed the phone to light suit. "Yes sir," was all grey suit said and handed the phone back.

"Sorry for the inconvenience Ma'am." Tim was released and the two MI6 operatives walked away.

Jeff looked at Elaine. "Waverly," she said. "He knew nothing about the whole affair, it seems that the orders are being issued by a section head. He will get to the bottom of it and keep us in the loop."

"Come with us Mr Burr," we should like to ask you a few questions.

Chapter 25

It was hot day in Istanbul and Annubis was beginning to feel the heat as he walked from the entrance of the Vezneciler metro station. The station was recently built and dedicated to death of the Ottoman police officers killed, when the British occupied the then Constantinople, in nineteen twenty. He walked slowly along the Street towards the Sehzade Mosque. The pavement was crowded and he was jostled as he made his way towards it. Annubis could not help admire the Mosque, clad in pink and white marble that seemed to glisten in the sun. The dome rose into the clear blue sky and the twin minarets and four subsidiary half domes gave the whole impression of a place of tranquillity in an otherwise chaotic city.

Annubis moved into the shade of one of the porticos. He contemplated praying, but he knew that there would be no peace to be found, neither in this life nor the next. His soul was corrupted beyond repair and there was no way forward until he had avenged the murder of his family.

He watched with a tinge of envy as the students made their way past, on their way to Beyazit Square, where Istanbul University's main campus was situated. He felt a deep air of sadness as he imagined that his younger brother would now be graduating and the pride of his Father and Mother at his doing so. Annubis knew that it had been his Father's greatest desire that his sons would follow him into medicine. It could now never come to pass and the hopes and the dreams of his family were now buried in the ashes of the conflict in Iraq and the perversity and cruelty of one man,

Mehmet.

He had been in Istanbul for over a week and had been following his target, getting to know his movements and his habits, getting to know the man, probing for his weakness. Mehmet was a hard target to attack. The spate of terrorist bombings over the preceding months had left the city in a state of high alert. Mehmet was no fool and had personal protection wherever he went. Two armed bodyguards shadowed his every move and anywhere he entered was checked ahead of him.

Despite the security surrounding him, killing Mehmet was not the problem. Annubis could have killed him countless times already. He had the skills and he had the weapon for the job. The conflict in Iraq and the PKK, the Kurdish insurgents in Northern Turkey, had ensured the easy availability of weapons to ISIS. His contact in Istanbul had supplied him with a Kalekalip KNT-308. This indigenous Turkish produced sniper rifle was a .308 calibre weapon and had an effective range of nearly half a mile. Annubis had used it successfully on a number of occasions for contract assassinations in the past.

ISIS simply wanted Mehmet dead in direct retaliation for the shooting of their operatives in London. Annubis needed so much more than just his death. He needed to set his mind to rest, to learn the details of his brother's death. For this he needed to be alone with Mehmet. He needed time to question him. Then and only then would it be time for Mehmet to die, Annubis knew that he would need a long time for that to happen.

The traffic was building up and the air thickened with the exhaust fumes. A queue of traffic had backed up despite the efforts of the policeman to get it moving. A bus was stuck in the line of stationary vehicles. Mehmet could plainly see that it was carrying about ten or twelve police officers. The driver was becoming increasingly irritated with the policeman on point duty, who seemed to be making matters worse the more he attempted to get things moving.

Mehmet was careful in his daily comings and goings. His training had become ingrained and he instinctively knew not to be a creature of regular habits and routines. His one weakness was the Hamam, the traditional Turkish bath house. Some days, in the late afternoon, Mehmet would go to a particular bath house in the Faith district about a half of a mile from where Annubis now stood.

The previous day Annubis had visited to reconnoitre the premises. He had left his clothes in the locker room and entered the hot and steam filled room. The bath house followed the normal routine. An attendant scrubbed him from head to toe with soapy suds, then rinsed him down with cold water in a side room with a basin. There was a deviation of significance. The final part of the routine is a massage where oil is rubbed into the body. It became apparent that rather attractive young men took some of the customers to private rooms. Given Mehmet's past history with himself and other boys at the orphanage, he had no doubt that this was the attraction that drew him to these particular baths. The plan was to be in the baths when Mehmet arrived and see if he had any preference or favourites among the young masseurs who worked there.

He left the shade of the Mosque and resumed his journey. The traffic had come to a complete standstill and a broken down car was being pushed to the side of the road by its two occupants. It was partially blocking the lane and tempers were beginning to flare. Horns were blaring and voices rose. The traffic officer was powerless to sort the mess. The bus containing the security police was stuck just yards from the broken down car. The policeman began shouting at the occupants to move the car.

The driver and passenger seemed to give up any effort at moving the incapacitated vehicle and suddenly started running towards the Mosque. The policeman screamed frantically after them as they disappeared into the crowd of tourists, worshippers and students. Enraged, he started to give chase. That saved his life.

The windows of the Mosque shattered as the blast wave hit the building. Annubis was thrown to the ground and was nearly deafened by the sound of the car bomb. When he staggered to his feet, he could see the bus was just a burnt out pile of steel and glass. The police on the bus had not stood a chance of survival, nor had the pedestrians and drivers of the cars surrounding the blast.

There were small pockets of fire lingering on the trees overlooking the road and smoke billowed upwards into the heavens. People were confused and shocked, unsure what had happened and unsure where to run. Often a second bomb would be planted by terrorists nearby and the fleeing crowd from the first blast would be fodder for the second. There was no second blast, it was clear that the Police bus was the target. The bombers had observed the bussing in and out of the security police and knew their route and shift pattern.

Annubis sat gathering his thoughts for a moment and raised himself to his feet. He checked himself out and was pleased to note that all the necessary bits still seemed to be attached to him. His ears rang and he had a bit of a headache, but apart from that, he was fine.

The sirens could be heard getting closer. Istanbul had been the centre for increased terrorist attacks both from ISIS and the PKK for some time. The emergency response to these incidents was becoming effectively coordinated and ambulances were soon arriving, the injured being treated and transported to the designated hospitals that were already rolling out their action plans.

The irony was not lost on Annubis, in that he had nearly been assassinated by ISIS who had just spent over a quarter of a million dollars employing him to carry out an assassination. He smiled as he made his way to the Hamam where he would await his targets arrival.

Chapter 26

The interview room in Thames house was pleasantly furnished with a table and four well-padded chairs. It had several video cameras mounted around the room that were of high quality, ensuring good sound and vision. Tim noticed that, unlike every interview room he had ever seen in police dramas on the television, there was not a large one way mirror on the wall.

Jeff Stiles formally introduced himself for the tape as did Tim.

Well Anthony, tell me all about it," said Jeff.

"My friends call me Tim."

"Alright, Tim we are your friends. I assure you," he smiled.

"It is a bit of a long story and it started when the Ambassador sent me off to pick up what was thought to be a bit of routine intelligence from a contact in the Turkish delegation."

Tim relayed the sequence of events that led up to the shootings in Wood Green, carefully avoiding mentioning that he and Yosuf had smuggled in a bucket load of heroin. Jeff was quick to pick up on the reason for them going to the Kebab House.

"Explain to me why you both went to North London?" asked Stiles.

"The arrangement was that they would sort a place for us to stay, a sort of safe house."

"And that is where you were going when the shooting kicked off?"

Tim nodded. Jeff seemed to be about to question the truth of the matter but realised there was no point in incriminating Tim by insisting on any further clarification of the matter, "You have handed over a print out of the memory stick and the stick itself. Do you have on you, or anywhere else for that matter, anything that might aid us further in this matter?" he asked.

"No," said Tim. He had decided not to mention the cash and cards that his wife held for him, nor the gun hidden in the hotel room. He also failed to mention the memory stick in his pocket showing Jason Delong's abuse and murder of the small boy. The conjurors trick had worked again when he had been searched, turning his pockets inside out with the stick hidden in the fold at the rear. He did not know why he lied to Jeff about these items. Something in him made him reluctant to tell all. He just had a feeling he may need them in the future, an insurance policy perhaps?

"What can you tell us about the contents of the memory stick?"

"It contains details of marine reinsurance policies placed by, what I suspect are insurance companies affiliated to or directly owned by ISIS or another similar terrorist organisation, or Countries that sponsor them. The Companies have effectively placed bets at odds of about one hundred to one that a ship over a certain size will sink in a twelve month period."

"I am still unclear."

"Say a ship over the target size sinks anywhere in the World, the bad guys would get paid, tax free by way of claims under these contracts, a billion or so US dollars," said Tim. "That money would flow into ISIS coffers, I assume."

Jeff's mouth dropped open for a brief second, "That much?"

"As far as I can calculate, but I am no expert. It is probably a lot more. I could not obviously run a check on the Insurers that benefit from these contracts but you, I assume, have the resource to check their provenance."

"We are doing this as we speak," confirmed Jeff. "But surely ships sink every day?"

"Of course but these bets have been placed on very big ships indeed sinking, such as a super tanker and they definitely do not sink every day That is why the odds these guys got on their bets were so high," said Tim.

"Fuck, are you saying ISIS could be about to attack and sink a super tanker?"

"I am afraid that is the conclusion I reached."

"Which one, where and how, do you know?"

"That is what we need to work out," said Tim.

He got up and headed for the door. "Don't just sit there, follow me." Tim caught up with him as he raced along the corridor and ignoring the lift started running up the stairs. Tim was glad that he had always kept up his training. They reached the top floor and continued to Elaine Wilkins' office. Jeff walked on, ignored the protest of the group of secretarial and admin staff and pushed the door open.

"What the hell is this," shouted Elaine, as they both barged in. She and the Home Secretary were sat at a coffee table with their cups of tea and a plate of biscuits. Both looked startled at the intrusion.

"Sorry, but I think you both need to be aware of this so please forgive me. This is Anthony Burr who was employed by this office to act as a liaison officer to the Paris Embassy." He said explaining the situation to the Minister. "Mr Burr has just revealed something to me in his debriefing, which I feel the Secretary should hear directly from the horse's mouth so to speak."

"Please," said the Minister.

Tim recounted his suspicions as to the imminent attack on a super tanker and the effect it would have on the fortunes of the terrorist's bank balances. There was a stunned silence in the room. The Home Secretary spoke, "I will inform the PM and recommend that he should call a meeting of COBRA. You had better let MI6 know the score. Keep me in the loop, no delay as soon as you know, I want to know," he gathered himself up and left with a wave.

"Sit," said Elaine.

"What about MI6?" Jeff asked.

"M denies knowing anything personally in their involvement, or lack or it in Anthony's adventure."

"Tim."

"What," said Elaine irritated.

Please, my friends call me Tim."

"I'll call you what the fuck I like," said Elaine, "Where was I? Don't' answer that either." She warned him. "It would appear that a junior Minister took it on himself to ignore the information about Yosuf and Tim." Tim kept his mouth shut.

"He didn't just ignore it. He passed information to the Turks," said Jeff, "Why?"

"We will never know officially. MI6 will sweep it under the carpet. It is pretty damn clear though that someone in the Foreign Office wanted the Turks to get credit for thwarting this for whatever reason." Tim knew the reason, Mailer, Delong's buddy covering his mates arse. He was also pretty sure MI6 knew the reason but were not going to embarrass themselves or the Government. Mailer would come to Paris and meet up with Jason and they would go off and party. Tim guessed what sort of parties these two enjoyed and it sickened him. More under carpet sweeping was about to take place.

"Do we hand this over to MI6?"

Elaine looked out of the window. Drizzle, June and drizzle she thought. Britain was heading for one of the wettest Junes in its history. "I think we should leave that for now, after all I distinctly heard the Minister say he was calling a meeting of COBRA and I shall brief the PM and other interested parties then. Well at least that is my understanding."

"That will not help our relations," observed Jeff.

"Well they shouldn't have left one of our operatives out in the cold, poor what's his name here, was left to his own devices. They should have come straight to us."

"Right," said Jeff. "You didn't even know he was on our pay role. Now you are suddenly offended by MI6's handling of him?"

"Tim," said Tim

She ignored him. "It is the principle of the thing."

"Which, principle is that then, the screw MI6 whenever you can principle?" Jeff laughed.

"Let's get this right. Take Tim here, sort out his background checks and upgrade his security level and decipher the rest of the information on the memory stick and find out where and when ISIS intends to sink this oil tanker." She said. "Go"

They went.

Tim found himself in a tiny office. There were people working in groups, but he could not join them or wander about until the security checks were completed. He found himself with limited access to files and the use of the internet. Tim looked around and wondered where all this was taking him. Only a week ago he had been having a jolly time in Paris and Monte Carlo. Since then he had been involved in gunfights, drug smuggling and murder. He had lost a friend and found himself becoming a spy.

He wondered what you did for lunch around here.

Chapter 27

Tim looked at the information he had gathered together while he waited for the code breakers to decipher the final part of the USB card. The stick had been sent to GCHQ and there was nothing to do but wait.

He had settled into a routine and had been staying at an MI5 flat while he looked for somewhere to live. He owned a flat in London, but he had rented it out when he was transferred to Paris. The lease still had over four months to run so he would have to rent himself until he regained possession. He had been interviewed, background checks done and he now had his security clearance. Things had moved quickly. He feared that he would be pushed into a backwater, but Jeff seemed to have taken a liking to him and had him reclassified. He had been promoted and had a salary increase. He was now just poorly paid, whereas before he had been piss poorly paid. He would need a lot more training, but that had been deferred for the present while they dealt with the immediate threat.

He was completing a background briefing for Elaine and Jeff that was more or less his old job at the embassy, so he was on firm ground. He also now knew a lot more about oil. There was a massive glut of oil, oil products and prices were at rock bottom. Oil tankers were backing up at the Euro Port in Rotterdam and the oil storage facilities there were full. The tonnage and capacity anchored in the North Sea waiting to unload was staggering. Some fifty tankers all with over two hundred and fifty tonnes were sitting idle.

The oil glut was also having an effect on the route taken by the tankers. The owners of the tankers were extending the voyage to avoid paying the cost of port fees. Ships coming from the Middle East have a choice of two routes. The first, a fifteen to twenty day journey through the Suez Canal or a forty day journey round the Southern tip of Africa, Cape of Aqulhas. Taking the longer route saved on the cost of the canal as well as dock fees. It also had the added benefit of giving the shippers more time to find buyers for their product.

Tim had spent several hours interviewing a broker to fully understand the information. For the first time he could actually say, "MI5, I should like to ask you some questions."

The political situation with Iran was also very fluid. The USA had imposed sanctions to pressurise Iran into falling in line on the development of nuclear weapons. A third of all oil in the World flows through the Strait of Hormuz, Iran's supreme leader had threatened to close it earlier in the year in retaliation.

The Strait of Hormuz is only twenty nine miles wide at its narrowest point. Its north coast is Iranian and to the south lies the United Arab Emirates. It provides the only access from the Persian Gulf to open ocean and is a natural bottleneck to the transit of the oil tankers. Blocking the channel would in many ways help the oil industry in general and clearly benefit the terrorists behind the "tonners" insurance policies specifically.

Tim left the building heading for Whitehall. He bagged a taxi and headed for his appointment with the Navel liaison officer, He was shown into a small office, a well-dressed young man about his own age introduced himself with a warm hand shake. Following an hour long meeting he was on his way back, armed with more detailed information as to what the Royal Navy was up to in the region.

"The Combined Maritime Force operates three Combined Task Forces in the region. CTF 150 covers the Hormuz Straits and CTF 151 is active in the Gulf of Aden. The former incorporates counter terrorism in its mandate while CTF 151 was established to deal with the threat of piracy, specifically from Somalia," said the Naval Officer.

Tim found out that the UK has four mine hunter ships on permanent deployment in the region, with an operation name of "kypion", as part of CTF 150. Its brief was to keep the sea lanes clear and the oil flowing through the Hormuz Strait. On the other hand CTF 151 was a multinational force. Command of CTF 151 is rotated between participatory nations on an approximately three to six month basis. CTF 151 is constantly changing as ships and aircraft from a variety of countries assign vessels, aircraft and personnel to the task force.

Tim sat and pondered. On the face of it, it looked like there was no way ISIS could sink an oil tanker at sea. It was crucial the ship was sunk at sea. If the tanker was docked the "tonners" policy would not pay. The ship had to be sailing or it was not a marine voyage policy.

The size of an oil tanker was prohibitive and the sinking of it with its compartmentalised hull made a total loss almost impossible, unless you had a submarine and Tim was pretty sure that ISIS did not have its own navy. His conversation with Navel Liaison also convinced him that, with the Combined Task Forces in the region, getting a ship close to a tanker would be exceedingly difficult.

He was stumped. He made his way to Jeff's office to update him. "Well! Where are we?" he asked.

Tim outlined his various meetings and the results. "So, basically nowhere," he said "I assume that when the USB stick is decoded it will give us enough information to identify their target ship, but on the face of it there appears that there is no practical way of dodging our Navy and even if you did, it would be almost impossible to sink a tanker with, say, a small boat."

"We are missing something, but what?" Just then he was alerted to an encrypted email from GCHQ. He studied it for a moment.

"We have our Tanker. The USB stick contained the navigational coordinates for a tanker. We have our boat and we know where it should be and when. The Nord Viking, nearly three hundred thousand tons, due to go through the Strait of Hormuz in seventeen days."

Chapter 28

The sign above the factory read "Northern Cross Inflatable proprietor: Razul Terzi". It was a busy place these days, employing nearly sixty people. Rasul had taken the business on from his Father and uncle. They had started the business making plastic inflatable boats for the beach, selling most of their product to the resorts in and around the coast by Bodrum. The area had been put on the holiday map and it had a mini boom.

Rasul had moved the business from essentially toys, boats and novelty beach items into making rigid hulled inflatable boats, known for short as RIBs. His factory was in Izmir, the third largest city in Turkey with coastal access. The impetus for the change of direction had been a meeting with Osman who had been looking for craft of any sort to smuggle the large volume of refugees and economic migrants to the Greek Islands.

Razul was not a stupid man and immediately saw the potential. He obtained a loan and set about expanding the business. He couldn't keep up with the demand, as Osman introduced more and more smugglers to him and was in turn paid a small commission on the sales that followed. Razul also had a side-line in importing cheap, knock off motors from China. The smugglers were not too worried about reliability and wanted to spend as little as possible. In essence, they just wanted the hull with no trimmings, like seats. They just wanted the inflatable ring and a cheap low powered engine. They crammed the boats full and pointed them towards the Greek Islands. They cared little, or not at all, for the safety of the occupants.

Razul, with the rapid expansion, had the foresight to look for further markets outside of Turkey for his RIBs. He could make the boats for about a third of the cost of the established manufacturers owing to his low labour and establishment costs. His breakthrough came in the Canadian market and from there to the US. So when Turkey came to a deal with the EU to stop the immigrants entering. he was no longer dependant on the illegal trade.

Razul had, if anything, taken on more orders than his business could cope with. He had a massive order for boats from Iraq, some forty two boats and they were to be equipped with top of the range motors, that they had also asked him to supply. These RIBS would be very fast indeed. The buyers had said they were for running tourists trips off the coast in the Gulf. Razul found this an unlikely explanation but left it at that.

The Iraqis had driven a hard bargain and he was making a minimal profit on each unit, so when he received a big order from his Canadian distributors, giving him a much larger profit, he had no hesitation in diverting some of the Iraqi order. They would just have to wait he decided. He had phoned them up and told them that he would be sending a part order by the due date and that fifteen boats would be delivered the following month. They had been unhappy and he had said they could take it or leave it, knowing that he could sell the rest of the boats at a higher price if they cancelled.

Two men, neatly dressed, approached the boatyard. They checked the sign to confirm they had the right address and entered. They pushed the door open to Razul's office and sat down on the chairs in front of him. He was taken by surprise and started to tell them he was a busy man and that he couldn't see them at the moment.

"We have come to discuss our order," said one,

"I have told you, I cannot make the delivery. You will just have to wait," he spoke in a condescending fashion as though lecturing children. "If you don't want what I can deliver you can cancel. I honestly don't care. You could sue me through the Turkish courts if you like. That is, if you have the odd ten years to spare," he smiled knowing he held the whip hand.

"We noticed that you are loading a number of your boats onto a truck. Where are they going?"

"That really is none of your business, but I do have other clients apart from yourselves."

"I see. We do feel that you should reconsider. It is obvious you have the boats we have ordered, but you are being greedy. are you not?"

"I am a businessman," Razul stated. "Now you know your options. Take it or leave it."

"Would you at least phone this number and speak to our boss and let him try to persuade you personally to change your mind." He placed a piece of paper with a mobile number on it on the desk between them."

Razul was now becoming extremely annoyed at the persistence of these idiots. "No I will not. Stop wasting my time and go before I have you thrown out."

"That may be harder to do than you think Mr Terzi." His companion casually withdrew a large pistol from his pocket and pointed it at Razul's face. "I suggest you stop wasting our time and phone that number."

Getting Razul's daughter to school had been the usual rushed affair for his wife. She had not taken her into the school itself as she was now twelve and liked to be grown up and wait for her friends and walk in with them. If she had looked in her rear view mirror, as she drove away, she would have seen her daughter being bundled into the back of the car that had followed her from their house that morning.

"Daddy, please daddy" his daughter sobbed. The phone went dead. The colour drained from Razul's face, he trembled as he looked up into the face of the gunman. He now saw what had been there to see all the time had he not been blinded by his own greed. These people were killers.

He got up. The gun clicked. "What are you doing?" asked the gunman.

"Stopping that truck leaving for the docks with your boats on it," he said. They followed him outside where he was just in time to prevent the trucks departure.

"You will get all the boats on time," said Razul, "my daughter?"

"She will be returned unharmed, when we have the boats. There is one final thing before that we need to arrange however."

"What?"

"As valued customers and given the fact that you have wasted a great deal of our time and put us through a lot of trouble, we think that a discount on our purchase is in order. Let us call it a gesture of goodwill on your part. You will deliver the boats and return fifty percent of the money we paid. We think we are being more than reasonable given the circumstances. As you said to us, take it or leave it."

He took it.

Chapter 29

Tim arrived at the conference room in the basement of MI5's building. He was surprised to find it crowded with staff on their lunch break. There was a large multi-screen television on the wall that the communications staff had kindly put up, linking the screens to form a cinema experience for the viewers to watch Wimbledon. There was silence when Elaine and Jeff, the head and deputy head entered. Jeff signalled for Tim to follow and they proceeded to the next room where a communications link had been set up with the CIA.

It was two in the afternoon in England and early morning in the US. The deputy director appeared on the screen and greetings were exchanged. "Mr Deputy Director, we have come into some information that we feel we should share with you" said Elaine. "I shall pass you to my colleague Mr Anthony Burr to brief you."

"We have received information that an oil tanker, the Nord Viking, is to be attacked by ISIS in the Strait of Hormuz in sixteen days. We have the exact time and location. The Combined Maritime Force patrols the region and the Task Force has been alerted. My understanding is that a private security force is aboard the Nord Viking and is in some strength. However, they are deployed to protect the crew and deal with a boarding. ISIS is not interested in taking the ship but sinking it and the attackers. They will not be concerned with their personal survival," Tim said.

"I am not clear why the sinking of one oil tanker is on their agenda. All our intelligence would clearly point to mass killings and bombings on soft targets?"

"Fund raising," Tim explained Tonners to the CIA man.

Following a long discussion between all the parties and a brief consultation with his advisors, the Deputy Director addressed them.

"Look, we have had a discussion here and it is pretty damn clear that the Iranians must be affording support if anything like this is to get close to success. We are, as you can understand, reluctant to get further involved after those Iranian shits took that boat load of US Sailors and we had to grovel to get the hostages back. Sorry folks, you are on your own in this one." He signed off.

"That went well," said Jeff,

"To be honest you can see their point of view. The ship is insured and it will be predominantly UK insurers that take the financial loss. Weigh that against getting embroiled in another Middle East conflict and I know where I would be on this if I were American."

Waverly, head of MI6, settled himself down with a biscuit and a cup of tea in Elaine's office. "Nice to hear from you again so soon," he smiled.

"As a matter of interest, did you get to the bottom of that bit of business in North London?"

"Yes, that, yes we did. Seems some junior Minister in the Foreign Office called in a favour from a friend in the London section. Rap over the knuckles all round, sorted now. Sorry for treading on your toes though."

Successfully brushed under the carpet thought Elaine, old boy network at its finest but held her tongue. "You have read the Intel on the Nord Viking and the likely threat?" she prompted.

"I agree, it is an MI6 matter, but I am not sure what we can do really."

"Send someone to get to the bottom of it and nullify the threat."

"There is not a great deal of appetite at the Foreign Office to get mixed up with the Iraqis and the Iranians. We have already had a fuck up there and do not really want to go back, thank you," he said.

"Pity we didn't apply the same logic to Afghanistan," quipped Elaine.

Ignoring the comment, Waverly continued," To be perfectly frank we don't have the budget or the resources to get involved. The Navy is there as part of CTF 150 and it must be left to them to deal with the threat."

Her next appointment was with the Home Secretary an hour later. It went along the same lines with the added statement that it was not a matter for MI5 as there was no threat to UK security. On the other hand, it would be greatly appreciated if she could somehow prevent the UK insurance industry taking a bath and avoid a financial meltdown.

"We drop it then," said Jeff.

"No real choice," replied Elaine

Chapter 30

Stiles had a busy few days. Ironically he found himself working closely with Mr Midas, John, the husband of Tim's ex-wife. He was chairman of the Lloyds' Marine Underwriters Association and he, along with the head of the International Underwriting Association London, represented virtually all those that stood to lose if the Nord Viking were to sink.

Stiles had arranged for both of them to sign and be bound by the Official Secrets Act. The problem was how to avoid paying a fortune to ISIS under the Tonnage contracts written by the members of the two Associations. They were given an office at Thames House to ensure security while a plan was devised.

"We could just cancel the contracts," suggested Sir Harry Fletch, Chairman of the IUA. Harry was a no nonsense bruiser who had worked his way up through the ranks of the world's largest insurance company outside the US. He was now a non-executive Director of several big companies as well as the Chief executive of the insurance company he had worked for all his life.

"You know we can't do that," said John.

There was no way of voiding the contracts. The contracts had been taken out in good faith and they would need positive proof that the insured were connected to the possibility of an attack on the Nord Viking. If such a connection to terrorist funding could have been established, these companies would have been part of an international ban. In any event, the ISIS threat could not be publicly revealed if they wished to avoid prosecution under the Official Secrets Act they had both just signed.

"We can easily reduce our exposure by reinsuring the risk into the US market," said John.

"That is not really the objective," said Stiles. "We do not want ISIS picking up billions of dollars, do we? I shall leave you gentlemen to come up with a solution that does not help ISIS profit from the sinking of the oil tanker." The two began to discuss matters and work through ideas.

In the meantime, Stiles walked to Tim's office. He found him looking rather depressed staring out of the window. "Cheer up," he said as he entered.

"Right," said Tim," It just seems such a bloody mess. People died you know, now we are going let that scumbag Mehmet, get away with it and probably let him claim the credit if we do manage to stop this plot."

"It is the nature of this business. We get our hands dirty so that everyone else can sleep safe at night. If we stop one bomb going off on a tube or bus we have done something worthwhile. "

"It is whole different moral perspective and I find it hard to adjust to. Take the CIA, they know people may die in the Nord Viking and that the UK based insurance companies could be paying billions of dollars into ISIS coffers, but still they wash their hands of it."

"Well, to be fair, the Foreign Secretary has made it pretty clear that we don't want to get entangled in it either."

"I am not saying that the USA is any worse than the UK, just that morality seems to have slipped off the agenda," said Tim.

"We are doing our best. I am sure those two will come up with a solution to the insurance problem."

"There's another issue. They are really no different to the bankers that gambled us into a global financial crisis. They have written a pile of dodgy contracts, that when you actually analyse it, are just a gamble on big ships sinking. It stinks. I get a pile of dosh, if it doesn't you get to keep my stake money. Now tell me what has that to do with insurance?"

"There is one bit of good news, Jason Delonge."

"What about him?"

"He's resigned, jumped before he was pushed and no Knighthood."

Tim thoughts strayed to the video he still had in his possession. Delonge was a paedophile and a child murderer and his punishment was to miss out on a Knighthood. He wanted to expose him, but he knew if he gave the USB stick to MI5 it would be quietly covered up. He knew, ultimately, he had to do something to get the bastard but, for now, he waited his time.

"That's something," he said.

The two esteemed leaders of the London marine insurance underwriters sat in Elaine's office "You have a solution? She asked

"We do and we think you will like it" said John.

"So tell me," she prompted.

"Here goes," said Harry. "We couldn't cancel the contracts as the British Courts would eventually force us to pay up. So we put together a contract of our own with John's Syndicate and my Company fronting it. We have contacted all the underwriters who have written the tonnage contacts and reinsured them with us so we have assumed one hundred percent of their risk."

Seeing Elaine looking a bit puzzled, John interrupted. "Our two concerns now have the sole liability to pay out if the Nord Viking or any other large ship sinks. All the rest of the market is off the hook and we offered them a small profit to ensure they all transferred the risk to us."

"I do not see how that really helps. To my mind your two businesses are still liable to pay these terrorist linked insurance companies billions. Are you not?" said Elaine

"That is correct, but we squared the circle, so to speak. We reinsured the total risk back with these same ISIS sponsored companies," said John

"Even better, due to what is called the reinsurance spiral effect, if and when they claim for the loss of the Nord Viking, we will be claiming about fifty per cent more from them," said Harry.

"Surely they don't have enough funds to pay you?" she said.

"Of course not, but it doesn't matter. We apply our right of set off. That is to say we deduct what we owe them from what they owe us and leave them owing a billion to us. We pass the money round amongst ourselves in the London market so no one gains or loses here."

"The bonus is that these dodgy, ISIS sponsored insurers go bust having paid up for the loss of the Nord Viking and are no longer able to launder money for them."

"Unbelievable, you really are as bad as the bankers," said Elaine.

"Well that is praise indeed. Thank you," laughed Mr Midas.

Chapter 31

Istanbul was as busy as ever and just as hot and clammy as anywhere could be. Annubis sat opposite the carpet shop. It was not a tourist shop with the fake Persian rugs imported all the way from India but of the domestic kind, with rolls of broadloom fitted carpet in the window. Just along the street was the colourful window of the material shop, with its rolls of highly patterned and vivid curtain and dress making fabrics on display.

Between the two shops was a gap over which a brick arch had been erected. It was a very tatty arch and looked like it would collapse at any moment, if it were not soon re-pointed. The sign to the left of the arch was in Turkish and read "Hamam", the sign on the left was in English and read "Turkish baths."

Annubis had identified that the only real opportunity to get to Mehmet without his bodyguards was on his regular visits to these baths. The problem being that, although his visits were often, they followed no pattern. He could not spend all day, everyday sat in the steam room on the off chance Mehmet would drop in. He had therefore formulated a different approach.

He waited outside the carpet shop until a young man walked through the archway. Seeing his opportunity, Annubis turned and bumped into him. The young man was about nineteen and delicately built with deep brown eyes and a very pale skin for a Turk. His body was taught and slim, his tight fitting T-shirt outlined the muscular definition of his torso. His slacks were off-white and tight fitting, emphasising the outline of his firm bottom and he wore soft beige leather moccasins. Annubis recognised the typical look of a rent boy from his own experiences when much younger. He had been forced into that way of life to survive.

"Sorry," he said, ensuring his gaze lingered on the young man.

The young man's gaydar kicked in and seeing before him a fit confident and very well dressed man in his late twenties, he responded with a smile. "Hi." Annubis found no difficulty in engaging him in conversation and he readily agreed to share a coffee. He took the young man to a very up market bar and made sure to give the impression of being a successful business man on a short trip to Istanbul. The conversation progressed easily and they parted with a date arranged for a night club later.

Annubis arrived at the Tekyon Club in Siraselviler Caddesi at one thirty and made his way to the rear garden area. He paused on route to watch the male belly dancers and, smiling, he made his way outside. The area was popular with smokers. A very effeminate waiter took his order and with a wiggle of his bottom disappeared in the direction of the bar. Baris, the masseur from the Hamam, waved as he spotted him in the garden. He came up to Annubis and flirtatiously kissed him lightly on the cheek.

The evening progressed with Baris introducing him to his mix of transgender and gay friends. For a brief period Annubis almost felt as a human being, but underlying his exterior there was no real warmth and no real depth of feeling. His was not homosexual, heterosexual or bisexual. He became what he had to become to do what he had to do.

The bears belly dancing was a site to behold. There was a small man in his twenties that was hairier than a real bear and his ability to wobble his body parts was spectacular. Baris and Annubis left the club laughing and managed to get a taxi back to Annubis' luxury hotel.

Annubis ordered champagne to be delivered to the room, even though it was past three in the morning. He poured Baris a glass and settled on the sofa. They toasted and sipped slowly. He lent in and placing his hand behind Boris's neck pulled him gently forward and kissed him. The kiss developed and passion rose. They got up from the sofa and headed to the bedroom.

The love making was passionate with Annubis taking the dominant role. Baris, satisfied and exhausted, fell into semi drunken sleep. Annubis silently rose from the bed and made his way to the lounge area where Baris's clothing lay scattered. He soon found Baris' phone. It was and old iPhone model. He scrolled through the call log and saw that Mehmet would phone to book his appointment directly with Baris. Annubis smiled.

They ate breakfast in bed and made love one more time. Annubis played the part of the smitten, rich businessman and Baris left mid-morning to return to his flat to change and then go in for his shift at the Hamam.

As soon as he left, Annubis dressed and calling a cab headed into Istanbul. His first port of call was the Apple Store where he purchased the latest, top of the range phone. He then took a taxi to a small electrical shop.

Annubis pushed the door open and entered. The bell on the door alerted the shopkeeper to his arrival. "Hello, my friend, I have not seen you in a very long time," said the owner. "You require something special?" Annubis handed him the phone.

That evening Annubis took a taxi to Baris's flat in a poor run down section of town. Baris ran from the flat to the waiting cab and settled in beside Annubis. They drove to a beautiful restaurant up in the hills overlooking the Bosphorus. Annubis had booked a table on the terrace. The setting was romantic with the Moon shining and looking down they, could see the bridge fully illuminated, the glow of the taillights of the cars heading east and their headlights as they headed west. No more clearly than at that moment did they feel that they were in a truly romantic setting where the World lay at their feet, the crossroads where Europe met Asia.

A small candle flickered on the table, half illuminating their faces. Annubis lent forward and took Baris's hand and looked into his eyes. He looked back and the affection in his face was plain to see. "I know we have only known one another for a short while, but I feel we have made an unique connection," said Annubis.

"I feel the same. You are very dear and special to me." Now whether Baris was playing Annubis for a sucker and stinging him along in the hope of milking a rich business man for all he could get was hard to determine. To Annubis, it mattered not in the least. He had no real interest in this young man, just in his connection to Mehmet,

He placed the gift wrapped box that he had held all evening on the table between them, "A little gift for you." Baris made all the right noises, no need, you shouldn't have and of course he took it anyway.

"I couldn't help noticing how old your phone was. It is fully charged. All you need to do is pop your sim card in it." Baris could not wait and unpacked the phone and inserted his card. When they returned to Annubis' room, Baris showed his gratitude in bed. The sex was long and hard.

In the morning, before Baris left for work, Annubis checked his phone. He was satisfied that all worked as well as his electronics friend had assured him it would. On the screen of his phone he could see all of Baris's texts, call logs and he knew he would be able to listen in to all the calls he made or received. He, of course, needed to be within range, but he would be when the time came.

Chapter 32

Tim had settled into his job at MI5 and was even beginning to find his way around the maze of corridors in Thames House. He had to admit that life seemed a little tame after his recent adventure, but his pay and grade was alright. He was assigned to assessing the threats posed from the Middle East and the various groups. The finale of his Turkish adventure had been to prepare an assessment of risk and exploration of the means that could or would be used by ISIS to attack the Nord Viking in the next few days and pass the available intelligence to the Navy.

He was angry that all the players had walked away relatively unscathed. Mehmet, was happily back in Turkey carrying on as normal. The Foreign Office had a little shake up with a junior Minister going. Jason was now employed by a multinational on a massive annual consultancy fee. The shooting in Wood Green had been passed off as the usual drug deal gone wrong. Yosuf was now forever branded as a drug dealer and not the real man that Tim knew. At least Tim would remember him as the true friend he was.

The paedophilia perpetrators, Mehmet and Jason would now escape any form of justice and be free to carry on as normal. A small boy raped and murdered would be forgotten along with so many other children suffering and abused around the Globe. What did it matter? They had no power and no one to speak up for them?

Tim was suffering from the inner torment of guilt and powerlessness. The cold and calculated way Mehmet had killed Yosuf played out over and over in his head. The look of shock and pain on his friend's face as he passed away just kept replaying in his head. The dreams were the worst of it. He would be running away from the firing, escaping. The means of escape was the nightmare. He would be running then he would be climbing an endless stairway to a pinpoint of light. He never got closer to the light as the stairway became soft and boggy. He would look down at his feet and see that the stairs were a mass of children's bodies that morphed into a pile of dead Yosufs.

He knew that he could not rid his mind of the images of Jason raping and killing the small boy with the Oval eyes. He picked up the phone and dialled the Premier Inn in Victoria where he and Yosuf had stayed.

"Hello, my name is Mr John Sparks. Do you have a room available for tonight? Yes, I do realise I can book on the internet. Yes, I know that there is an online discount but I am not on the internet, I am on the phone," he was becoming irritated and took a deep breath. He did not want to antagonise the anonymous voice on the other end of the phone. He needed to get her onside.

"I wish to stay in a particular room. I do understand that they are all the same quality with new upgraded mattresses for a sound night's sleep, but really, I would like a specific room." He managed to keep his frustration under control as everything he said was met by a scripted reply that, it was clear, the operator was reading slowly from a computer screen in a monotone.

"I should like to book into room twenty two," he persisted. The operator explained that the central booking system did not allow her to allocate specific rooms, but she could confirm his reservation by email and then, if he contacted the hotel and spoke to the manager, he might be able to arrange something.

Tim booked the room and phoned the hotel. The same mantra was repeated by the voice at the end of the phone." I am sorry the computer allocates the rooms and handles all aspects of the booking experience." The same system, the voice added "was award winning."

"Which room am I in anyway?" he said in frustration.

There was a pause, "Just a moment while I check, Sir," came the reply, "Number twenty two." Tim resisted the urge to scream or swear and clicked the phone off.

The day dragged and Tim found himself not concentrating on the work in hand but instead, thinking of the course of action he was contemplating embarking upon. What he was about to do contravened his whole image of himself. Did he have the moral authority to make this decision? Was he really a man that should make a life and death decision? Was he plagued by self-doubt, revenge or justice?

Finally, it was time to leave work. The distance to the hotel was relatively short, but the crowded platforms and pavements made the journey time disproportionate. He finally struggled up the Street and entered the lobby. He handed over his fake credit card in the name of Mr Sparks. Just one of the many cards Yosuf had unintentionally bequeathed him. He stood there and took a deep breath. He felt the next step he would take would change his way of life forever and change him as a person. He calmed himself and walked to the stairwell.

The walk along the corridor brought memories flooding back of his lone return, here with blood spatter on his clothes and his person. He felt his legs seemingly grow heavier as he walked to room twenty-two. He inserted the key card and entered. He stood still in the middle of the room. The curtains were drawn and a small shaft of light penetrated the semi gloom. He stood as before looking at the patterns the small dust particles made as they swilled up and down.

He had stopped at a Robert Dyas, the hardware store on his way here and bought a screwdriver. He removed it from his pocket and waked to the bathroom. This time he was equipped with the right tool and soon unscrewed the access hatch in the tiling. He reached in and felt the Makarov, cold and heavy in his hand. He retrieved it and placed it in his jacket pocket.

He left the hotel and felt the weight of the gun in his pocket and the weight of his decision in his heart. The die was cast and he knew he needed to do this, but it was with the sense that he might just be adding to the sum total of evil in the world.

Chapter 33

Captain Stanley Jones sat at the head of the boardroom table with the first officer and staff of HMS Defender. He had in front of him the briefing from MI6. The Steward finished serving a round of coffees. Jones was self-assured confident and in his early forties, fit with dark brown hair and an intelligent looking face, that at this moment carried a deep frown as he studied the documents in front of him.

"Gentlemen, it would seem, if this briefing is correct, that there is to be a terrorist attack on an oil tanker as she passes through the Gulf." He read the details of the proposed attack on the Nord Viking. "She is pulling into port as we speak to begin loading her cargo of oil." HMS defender, a type 45 destroyer, with a compliment of just over one hundred and ninety crew, was one of the most advanced air defence ships in the world. In addition to its Sea Viper air defence system, its array of guns, ranging from a 4.5" Mark 8 Mod to six general purpose machine guns, had the capacity to fly two Lynx HMA8 helicopters. It was powered by two Rolls Royce gas turbine engines.

"Engines first," he said.

"Fine at the moment." replied the Chief Engineer, "but we need to be mindful of any dramatic increases in external temperature." The engines had a problem in coping with the heat in the Gulf, had a history of breaking down and poor performance.

"Let us turn to how we propose to respond to this bit of

intelligence," said Jones. There were a number of options available. HMS Defender could sail north and escort the Nord Viking all the way south through the Hormuz Strait and onward, it could stay in the vicinity of the Strait until its arrival, finally it could continue routine patrols and rely on its speed, of approximately thirty knots, to respond rapidly to any threat.

"How confident are we in the source of the intelligence? I cannot see how any terrorist group would have the capability to significantly damage the tanker, let alone sink it. The construction, double skinned as it is, is a formidable barrier to sinking it and this report shows that the owners have hired a large private security force on border to shepherd it through the Gulf," said the First Officer.

"MI6 stress the immediacy and credibility of the threat, but do not give any indication on how the attack is to be mounted. If we were dealing with Somali pirates, the attackers would try and board the vessel and take control. In this instance the object is to sink her. They could still attempt a boarding and plant explosives," said Jones.

"It would be easier to plant a bomb or attach explosives to her hull while she is docked, surely?"

"Security is very high at the terminal and well established. It would be virtually impossible to get a device into the port and getting it aboard even harder. In any event, we are not concerned with ships in port, we deal with the maritime threat," said Jones.

"I honestly cannot see how a tanker of that size could be sunk by a small group of terrorists in a small boat, or a big boat for that matter. I mean this is one hell of a big bit of floating metal. You would need to torpedo it. No group has the means to do that."

"I have to admit, I would dismiss this if it wasn't for the credibility of the threat the Secret Service attaches to it. I accept that, on the face of it, no group has the capability to prosecute such an attack, but we do need to treat it as a credible threat and consider our response."

"Exploring our options, if we sail north we leave this area under resourced. What is the likely outcome?" asked the Intelligence Officer.

"Not much really, the smugglers bringing goods into Iran would just have a bit of an easier time sanction busting, I suppose," Jones replied.

"We could stick to our routine pattern of patrolling."

"I am not overly enamoured with that option. If they do damage or sink the bugger, I should not like to stand in front of a Board of Inquiry and in answer to the question, 'how did you respond to the threat?' and give the answer," nothing, we carried on as usual"."

"Not good," agreed the first officer.

"We hang about in the Strait and wait for her."

"It looks a bit passive. 'What did you do asks the Board?' My answer, we sat about waiting."

"Summing up then," said Jones, "we don't think there is a cat in hells chance of the Nord Viking being sunk, unless the terrorists have bought a submarine. On the other hand, we know we should ignore it and maintain our presence, but we are fearful that even if the bloody thing manages to sink itself, by crashing into the dock or running itself aground, we would end up being blamed."

"What are your orders then?" asked the first officer.

"Let's play baby sitter. We sail to meet and escort her."

Two hours later HMS defender was steaming north, Jones was on the bridge. He was drinking a mid-morning cup of tea and enjoying a chocolate biscuit as he gazed out across the Gulf. He had to admit, this was the best job ever, boys dream of sailing their own warship about.

"Captain, we've picked up the "Rust Bucket." The Rust Bucket, not the real name of the vessel, was a regular customer of the Defender. She was a cargo vessel of around thirty thousand tons and usually up to no good, smuggling something or someone without the correct paper work.

"It's her lucky day, maintain the heading," said the Captain.

Chapter 34

The temperature on the tarmac was scorching as the plane from Tehran touched down at Baghdad airport. The flight had been on time leaving, the landing however was not. There was an incident at the airport described as a security alert. Since the retaking of Fallujah from ISIS, they had been determined to demonstrate that they were still a force to be reckoned with. The outcome was that the magnitude and severity of the bombings in the Capital had intensified.

Earlier in the month, coordinated bombing attacks had been made across the city and casualties were large. A truck bomb had killed more than two hundred and fifty people when it exploded in the Karrada district, where the population was mainly Shia Muslims. The bomb went off at midnight when the area was crowded with shoppers breaking their Ramadan fast.

Professor Javadi looked at the reports in the newspaper handed to him when he boarded and a small smile crossed his lips. He was a small man in his late fifties and wore thin rimmed glasses. His teeth were stained from smoking, as were the tips of the fingers where he held the cigarettes. He was a heavy smoker and was feeling the effects of nicotine depravation as he waited to get off the plane..

They did not disembark immediately, but were kept waiting on the apron for a further forty minutes. The temperature in the plane started to rise as the sun beat down on the fuselage. He really felt he needed a cigarette as he stewed in the plane's interior.

Thirty six years ago, Professor Javadi had been a student and spent over a year occupying the US Embassy in Tehran. The Shah had been overthrown and the Americans were humiliated. He and his fellow students had taken control of the Embassy and held fifty two American diplomats hostage.

An attempt to rescue the hostages, led by the then President of the US, Jimmy Carter, had been a complete catalogue of errors and resulted in the deaths of eight American military personnel before they even set foot on Iranian soil. It sealed the fate of Jimmy Carter's political career, he did not run for re-election in 1980.

The occupation of the embassy defined and influenced the relationship Iran had with the West for decades. Javadi remembered being on campus listening to the speeches and rhetoric of the student leaders. The Shah had been a puppet of the West, lining his pockets and living the life of an international playboy, supported and put in power by the great powers of the day. In effect, they kept him in power and in return he let them rape the Country of its natural resource, oil.

This was the era of the "student sit in" as a means of protest. Students would occupy various buildings and just stay there until the authorities gave into their demands or managed to remove them. The students marched on the Embassy to protest with a "sit in" planned over the Shah being given sanctuary in the West. They demanded his returned for trial. The "sit in" lasted for four hundred and forty four days and became increasingly more militant under the guidance of the religious leader, Ayatollah Khomeini.

Javadi eventually finished his education and went on to great things. He was now a leading light in the Iranian nuclear programme, internationally renowned and respected in the field. He was also fervent in his fundamentalist beliefs and irreconcilable hatred of the West.

Eventually the steward gave the order to disembark. Javadi rose from his seat and banged his head on the overhead locker. With the yearning to smoke, the delay and now hitting his head he was in a foul mood by the time he reached the baggage reclaim area. After nearly an hours wait for his bag to turn up, he was in an even worse mood as he left the airport building.

On exiting, he immediately reached in his pocket and lit a cigarette. Having not had his nicotine dose in nearly seven hours he felt slightly giddy as he took his first drag. He had not experienced this effect from a cigarette since his was thirteen years old, feeling very grown up as he took an illicit puff on his elder brother's cigarette.

Following the occupation of the American Embassy, Javadi had managed to resume his studies and obtained his physics degree in Iran. His doctorate was a laboured affair and it took him nearly five years to complete. The climate for study had not been easy with the constant political turmoil, that often halted academic life completely. He finally completed his PhD and began work in the coveted atomic weapons programme.

Although the Americans had sanctioned the Iranians in every way possible to halt their nuclear programme, he had become a well-respected figure in the Global scientific community and was welcomed worldwide at academic forums and conferences, both as a contributor and as an attendee. He was here in Baghdad to attend just such a conference. The Government, despite the total lack of control it held over the security of the country, was trying, not wholly successfully, to restore some sense of normality to its educational and research institutions. The conference had been organised by the faculty of science headed by a professor Azizi.

The driver of the black Mercedes was forced to wait while Javadi finished the last of his cigarette. He put Javadi's suitcase in the car's boot and busied himself by wiping the wing mirrors. He was obviously anxious to get a move on, but Javadi was not to be rushed. Javadi would have smoked in the car, but he knew that the

University was pandering to international standards and avoiding the dangers of passive smoking for its staff. This thinking, Javadi thought, was somewhat spurious, given the constant danger of being shot or blown to bits.

Javadi looked from the window of the car at the dusty scene. The whole area had been the subject of a constant onslaught by the militia when the British troops had been forced to retreat to the airport. The roadside and buildings still bore the scars of the bombings and mortar attacks. The reconstruction was slow and the city still had the resemblance of a war zone. The car got caught up in a queue for a Government check point and he was again forced to sit and wait. He wound down the window and lit another cigarette. The driver looked disapprovingly at him in the mirror for potentially dirtying the inside of the car. Javadi stared defiantly back at him.

The driver opened the back rear door and handed him his suitcase. He then made a point of leaning into the back and wiping a particle of cigarette ash from the seat before shutting the door and driving off.

"Welcome my friend, I am so glad to see you again," said professor Azizi.

The suitcase was picked up by a third man who accompanied Azizi as they made their way to an office. "Well, what is the plan?" asked Javadi.

"I have put about to my colleagues and anyone interested that you and I are going fishing."

"Fishing?"

"It was the best I could do and it does account for our absence. Anyway, it sort of fits you as a slightly eccentric academic, don't you think?" said Azizi.

The pickup was waiting for them as night fell. The power had failed and the whole area was in total darkness as they left the city. With no light to pollute the heavens, the stars filled the night sky. The landscape was barren as they travelled further way from the population centre. Eventually, they arrived at a group of buildings. There was a small compound and a small industrial complex that had obviously been used as a military base at some stage, given the number of bullet holes in the brick work. Lights were on as electricity was being manufactured by the emergency generator.

Javadi's suitcase was taken to his sleeping quarters and he and Azizi were accompanied by an armed guard, one of many in and around the compound, to a canteen area. Javadi lit a cigarette and was introduced one by one to the people who were to be his colleagues for the next few days.

"Let's look at the facilities," suggested Azizi.

They entered a large work space, fully equipped with all the machinery Javadi had requested. "Amazing, how did you put all this together?"

Azizi laughed and shrugged his shoulders." Money talks here, as it does in most places and if that doesn't work, we have the barrel of a gun."

"We need to get to work. We do not have much time and although it is not that technically challenging, we need to do it right," said Javadi.

"We have everything we need and now we have you. The nuclear material is of varying grades, but we have more than enough our purposes"

"Well my friend, it will be a toss-up for you as to if you get cancer from secondary smoking or from radioactive contamination. Let us build the bomb," laughed Javadi.

Chapter 35

Annubis was in a philosophical mood as he drank his morning coffee in the hotel room. Baris had left to go back to his flat before going into work at the Hamam. On the face of it, their budding romance was in full flow, but the truth was far different.

The phone was doing its job and allowing him to track all Baris' movements, texts and conversation. Despite his claim to be a free agent, Baris had a long term boyfriend with whom he kept in constant contact. Annubis was known as the rich business man and his affection for him was to be used to extract all that could be extracted, legally and illegally. They were pleased with their haul so far, clothes, gifts and the iPhone, but they were hoping to get more.

Annubis listened to the plot to rob him of cash and cards before he was due to leave. Baris was trying to glean as much information as he could, in the hope of doing a bit of identity stealing. He could not, of course, know that Annubis' identity was a mere fantasy and one of many he had and would use. He was not in the least surprised at Baris' duplicity as he had done far worse to survive and was, of course, in the business of doing the worst full time job, killing people for money.

It was a moot point as to who was using who. Annubis was only interested as a way of getting to Mehmet and considered a few gifts to a gay prostitute well worth the investment. He surmised, as he finished his coffee and began to dress, that everyone uses everyone in some way.

He finished buttoning his shirt when the phone rang, that is to say the call monitoring Baris' iPhone alerted him to an incoming call. He listened to the voice on the phone, a voice he had not heard since he was fourteen years old. For a brief moment he felt the fear again. The fear of a small boy waiting for his abuser to collect him in the knowledge that he had no choice, that he was to be used as a sex toy for this man and his friends. The fear surprised him. He had felt so little in the years that proceeded this moment so to have that strong an emotion was truly dislocating, albeit just for a brief instant. The fear gave way almost instantaneously to sheer hatred and loathing. He felt the blood lust. He could taste it and savoured the pleasure of the anticipation of watching this piece of scum die.

At three that afternoon was when Mehmet would require Baris' services. At last Annubis would know where Mehmet would be and more to the point, he knew that he would not have the protection of his goons. At one point Annubis had feared that Mehmet had lost interest in the twink at the Turkish baths but apparently not. He was explaining to Baris that with all the bombing in Istanbul it had been all hands to the pumps and he had been drafted in to boost the security forces. His abstinence had in fact increased his lust and he was explaining to Baris what he was to provide that afternoon in the most graphic of detail.

Annubis settled the hotel bill with a credit card that was untraceable and would never be used again and stored his luggage. He then made his way to the Hamam, arriving an hour and a quarter before Mehmet, thus ensuring he would be inside before Mehmet arrived.

He entered the room wearing his towel and tried to relax in the steam. He felt different. He usually felt little emotion, but this was almost a new experience for him, anticipation or perhaps excitement? It had started as he had passed through the dilapidated brick archway between the carpet and the fabric shops. He had waited all his life to get the bastard who had taken his brother

168

away, never to return. It was so close. He forced himself to remain calm as Mehmet entered the steam room.

Mehmet seemed to fully relax as he let the steam cleanse him. He was in no hurry and lent back with thin rivulets of sweat on his body. Annubis concentrated on the building. It was old, made of marble and granite, the ceiling, cavernous, supported by an array of pillars from which large brass chandeliers hung on chains. It had been a very opulent place to come and socialise in its heyday. Now, it was a bit care worn, almost grubby.

Mehmet was being washed down by a very overweight attendant with soapy water that was taking the sweat and impurities from his body. He looked at his watch and saw it was nearly time. He rose unobtrusively and made his way to the shower before he entered the locker and changing room.

The locker room was off the corridor that led to the private rooms used to provide the services offered by the young men that worked here. From here Annubis could see the coming and goings through the slightly opened door. He opened the locker that was full length and took his clothes from the hanger along with a gift wrapped box. He dressed and positioned himself to keep watch. He saw Baris enter the third door along carrying a bundle of white towels and a large glass bottle containing scented massage oil. He ducked out of view as Baris went off to collect Mehmet from the baths.

Annubis, through the crack, could see Mehmet, followed by Baris, heading to the massage room. He allowed him to pass and quietly opened the door so that Baris could see him holding the box wrapped in silver paper. Baris smiled and put his fingers to his lips in a gesture of silence. Annubis smiled back and watched as Mehmet entered the room. Baris said, "I have forgotten something. Go in and make yourself comfortable," he turned and retraced his steps to the locker room, eager to see what Annubis had bought him this time.

Annubis signalled Baris to enter the locker room. He closed the door. "For you," He handed the box over to Baris. He started to unwrap the gift, "First a kiss?"

Baris moved his face close to Annubis and their lips touched. Annubis placed his hands either side of Baris' face and caressed him as they kissed. Then, with a quick twist of both his hands, he snapped his neck with a loud crack. Annubis looked into his startled face as he watched him die.

Even for one as fit as Annubis it was a struggle to lift the body into the locker, but he managed to accomplish it. He picked up the gift wrapped box that had fallen from Baris' hands during in his death throes. He pulled off the paper, lifted the lid and took his gun from the box. He checked the locker and closing the door behind him, made his way to the massage room.

He checked that the corridor was empty and gun in hand, he entered the room. The room was small with a basin in one corner and a massage bed in the centre. Mehmet was lying face down the table, naked with his head through the hole provided. "You were a long time," he said, as Annubis entered. There was a key in the door. It was large and antiquated. Annubis turned it so avoiding any unexpected disturbance.

Standing behind Mehmet, Annubis removed his jacket and rolled up his sleeves. He took the glass bottle of oil and poured a small quantity of it onto the nape of Mehmet's back. He gently rubbed the oil into his buttocks, Mehmet writhed slightly from side to side. He was becoming aroused in anticipation as Annubis slowly slid his hands to his shoulders. He readied himself and surprising Mehmet, he placed his knee in the small of his back.

His full weight was on him, pinning him to the table. In one swift movement his put his left arm round his neck and locked it in place by placing his right arm behind his neck and putting his hand in the crook of his elbow. By pushing forward he could have snapped

Mehmet's neck, but he did not want a swift death for this man. He instead applied enough pressure to stem the flow of blood to his brain. They sat locked together in that position, with Mehmet struggles growing slowly weaker until he slipped into unconsciousness.

Mehmet opened his mouth and tried to shout, he couldn't as his mouth was full of towel. He tried to move but he couldn't as he was tied to the table. He focused his eyes and saw a young, powerfully built man, big oval eyes with his sleeves rolled up pointing a gun at him.

"Welcome back," said Annubis, "I doubt that you remember me, but we have met. I was much younger then and you and your friends used to take turns in buggering me and forcing me to suck your dicks. Ring any bells yet?" Fear spread across Mehmet's face.

"Ah, I see it is coming back to you. You used to collect us in your lovely big shinny car, give us sweets then rape us. That's it. You have it now. I was one of the boys you used. I am here to repay the favour and ask you a few questions. Now I shall take the towel out of your mouth. Obviously, if you shout or scream this conversation will come to a speedy conclusion as I shall use this, rather big, gun to blow your brains out, do you understand?"

He removed the towel and Mehmet took in a deep gulp of air. He started to speak, to protest, Annubis shoved the barrel of the gun into his mouth forcing him to gag. "I want only one thing from you. A boy was murdered during one of your little parties. All I want to know is, who was responsible? Did you kill him or if not, who did?"

"You are confused I know nothing about any of this," Mehmet started to protest. "I warn you, I am a very powerful man and you will pay for..,"

Annubis pushed his gun back into Mehmet's mouth," I must stop you there. I know who you are and in your current situation I do not think any of that is relevant." He picked up the glass bottle filled with oil and positioned it above Mehmet flaccid penis. He tapped the neck of the bottle with the butt of his gun until it smashed, leaving him holding the neck with a jagged serrated edge. The oil emptied from the bottle onto his member. Annubis massaged the oil in to his penis, gently at first then grabbing his testicles he applied all his strength to crush them between his fingers.

"Now, I should like you to experience what I felt when you used me." Without warning he rammed the broken bottle into Mehmet's anus. He rotated it as he pushed. Like a drill it cut as it went deeper, he pushed and turned deeper and deeper. Blood spurted and bits of soft tissue ripped from the gaping, bleeding mess.

Holding the towel over Mehmet's mouth, he waited patiently while his screams subsided. "Hurts don't it?"

"Now tell me about the night you took the boy away."

Mehmet was shaking with fear and pain. "It was not supposed to happen. One of the guests got carried away."

"You?"

"Not me, no, no, not me, you have to believe me." He whimpered. The pool of blood was spreading across the massage table and dripping onto the floor. Annubis was careful not to step in it as he questioned him.

"Who?"

"A man called Jason Delonge. His is now a British diplomat."

"Only him?"

"Yes, yes, only him," Mehmet was becoming desperate as the blood spread.

"Thank you," said Annubis and reaching down pulled the broken bottle neck from what had once been Mehmet's anus.

He took the bottle and using it like a saw cut away the end of Mehmet's penis. He took a quick step back as the blood spurted and avoided getting covered. Mehmet tried to scream. Annubis brought the butt of his gun down into his open mouth, smashing his front teeth to fragments. He pick up the tiny pink mess that once had been Mehmet's penis and placed it in his bloody, broken tooth, filled mouth. Mehmet passed out. "You won't need one of those again," he said

He removed the feather from his wallet and placed it on Mehmet's body, "A soul heavier than a feather." He moved to the sink and washed the blood from his hands as he watched Mehmet slip into unconsciousness and die. He locked the door and left.

He was at the airport and leaving the country three hours later. He was also a lot richer as ISIS transferred the money for the hit into his account. A win, win situation he thought as he ate the, somewhat tasteless, meal served to him on board the plane.

Chapter 36

The calm sea reflected the light with such intensity from the surface of the Gulf's waters that it dazzled. Points of silvery light danced on the almost totally still sea, only stirring here and there with the small puffs of the breeze. The Nord Viking was preparing to sail. From the bridge, the Captain and crew could make out the bow and stern in the distance. The surface of the water was far below them. The size of the tanker was awe inspiring. The power of the engines astronomic and the weight of the vessel with its cargo was mind blowing. All figures so large that they were hard to envisage or truly take in.

Despite the fact that it was truly a Leviathan of the seas, it was easier to sail than a little dingy used for weekend jaunts on a lake. The wheel house did not have a wheel. The bridge would be more a home to a computer gamer or a city forex trader than an old school sailor. The computers were there constantly checking the operation of the vessel, its health, navigating and responding to the small movements of a joystick. The system, if on an aircraft, would be called "fly by wire", this was, however, "sail by wire." Its aim was to minimise the risk of human error and avoid the disastrous consequences of a major oil spill.

The captain and its crew had been briefed on the possible terrorist threat. It hardly seemed possible, the captain was totally unconvinced as to its credibility. Naturally, if ISIS had access to a warship, the threat would be possible to prosecute, but one thing was certain, they did not have a navy. Even if they did, it would have to be a pretty sophisticated one to overcome HMS Defender that was providing their escort.

The tanker was designed, as are all ships, to make it very difficult to sink. It was, effectively, double hulled and was sectioned into water tight compartments. Even if the hull was breached it would still remain afloat and the oil would be contained. Of course, collisions occur all the time with ships and jetties. Captains or pilots get it wrong and bash into the quayside and while the damage to the jetty and vessel can be expensive, it rarely causes any risk to a ship. The Nord Viking was, despite its immensity, very manoeuvrable. Its system of thrusters allowed it to move not only forward but sideways and any combination in between. No, the captain could not envisage this ship being sunk.

There was always the danger of a boarding and bombs being brought aboard. The Somalis had past successes in boarding tankers. However, that was before, when the security personnel were unarmed and only had basic equipment, like water cannon to repel potential boarders.

While the captain dealt with the pile of paper work needed before they could put to sea, a jeep pulled up quayside. It carried five individuals, who were the sort of individuals you would wish to avoid if you were contemplating getting into a fight. They were led by ex-sergeant Bootle, ex commando and now security consultant. The other four were all former military and naval personnel. Their backgrounds ranged from the Special Boat Service to the Marines, all professional and all highly trained. Fully kitted and with modern weapons, they were a formidable, efficient and fully trained tactical unit that could easily be sent in to deal with any situation, A lightly armed group of Somali pirates would find it neigh impossible to out fight or out manoeuvre this group of men. The vessels owners were doing their best to protect their investment.

The security force boarded the ship and having stowed their gear, they began surveying the ship. They had studied the vessel's plans prior to boarding and now did a physical exploration. Bootle was granted permission to enter the bridge and he settled down with the Captain to discuss their response to a potential armed boarding. The security force had been thorough and Bootle was clear and concise in his instructions to the Captain. He finished by saying, "In essence, we need you and the crew to keep well out of the way if it kicks off. The last thing you or we need is anyone getting in the line of fire. Gather the crew on the bridge and lock the ship down. We can defend and defeat a small army if they attempt a boarding."

Formalities cleared the Nord Viking finally put to sea.

The HMS Defender was lying to the south and waiting for the tanker to make headway in to the Persian Gulf. She would effectively scout ahead of the Nord Viking and await her arrival in the Hormuz Strait. She would then shepherd the tanker through and then return to routine patrol.

"Nice weather," said the First Officer

"It is indeed," replied Captain Jones. They were taking a stroll on deck and enjoying the morning air. A flock of gulls had gathered above them, sensing that there may be a meal for them as the chefs cleared the remains of breakfast. "See that this gull shit is cleared up, will you?"

"It looks like it is going to be a scorcher again today," continued Jones. Even for the Gulf it was hot and set to get hotter.

They wandered into the bridge. "The Nord Viking has set sail, Captain."

"About time, let's go and take a look. Get her underway," said Jones.

After an hours sailing they saw the tanker. "Well, she is easy enough to spot, I doubt if even the worst sailor could miss that." HMS Defender sailed ahead and to the east of the tanker as they made their stately procession towards the Strait.

Further down the western seaboard, just round the point at Kumzar in Dubai, the Golden Crescent, also known to the Defender's crew as the SS Rust Bucket, lay anchored. HMS Defender had seen her as she sailed north, but familiarity breeds contempt and they had totally ignored her presence, assuming she was up to her usual, no good, bit of smuggling. There had been a few modifications made to the vessel recently. A gantry and three small hoist type cranes had been added to the deck. The design was such that cargo from the hold could be lifted and lowered overboard into the sea. A platform had been installed at water level, accessed by rope ladders to allow easy boarding onto a smaller boat or dingy.

On the bridge, the Captain looked on the radar. There were, of course, many boats of all shapes and sizes. He had however become pretty good at tracking the Defender, in order to avoid it during the course of their smuggling activities and it wasn't going to be too hard to spot the monster tanker when she arrived. All was ready. All they had to do was wait.

The Defender was a few nautical miles ahead of the Nord Viking as they entered the Hormuz Strait. They were on full alert. There was a lot of shipping activity, most of which they identified and discounted as a threat

"This looks like a bit of a waste of time."

"Just do your job Lieutenant," said the Officer of the watch.

The Captain took control of the bridge, "Anything?"

"No, nothing, SS Rust Bucket is still moored just off the point. It appears to be broken down or up to no good, but not of interest at the moment."

The Nord Viking began its passage through the strait and passed in front of the Rust bucket obscuring her from view. At that point, the rigid hulled inflatable boats began their assault. There were forty of them lowered from the deck of the Rust Bucket and manned with two Jihadist per dingy. They appeared like a swarm of beetles racing across a dung pile in the binoculars of the watchers on HMS Defender.

"What they hell is that?" pointed Jones as he saw the mass of black dots stream into view, heading at high speed for the tanker. These types of boat were popular with Special Forces all over the world. They, as the name implied, had a rigid glass fibre hull surrounded by an inflatable collar, RHIBs for short. They were light, fast and highly manoeuvrable and ideal as assault craft.

About thirty of the RHIBs headed after the Tanker and fifteen or sixteen were on a direct course to HMS Defender, They were closing at a speed of nearly sixty miles an hour. The two men in each boat were bouncing across the waves, clinging on as best they could. The Defender compliment ran to their stations and began firing at the oncoming boats. The boats darted from side to side, weaving as they approached. The bigger guns were not designed for this and the light and medium machine guns were best suited to the task, spraying a line of continuous fire at the massed horde of boats flying towards them.

"Get us up to full speed. We need to get between the Nord Viking and the boats heading for them." The sheer number of dinghies had shocked him. He feared that they could actually manage to board the Tanker. HMS defender herself was under threat. Hand held rocket propelled grenades, RPGs, were being fired at them as well as machine gun fire.

Suddenly they slowed to a crawl. "Shit," said Jones. He didn't need to be told what had happened. The engines had overheated. The Rolls Royce engines just could not cope with the heat in the Gulf. The newspapers had been full of the story. HMS Defender became a bystander, The Jihadist soon realised that they were going nowhere and abandoned the diversionary assault and headed off to join the attack on the Tanker.

Chapter 37

Sergeant Bootle was on the deck of the Nord Viking. Even he was surprised at the force heading towards them. Initially around thirty dinghies were launched towards them at high speed and now more were coming their way, having been released into the fray with the breakdown of HMS Defender. As far as he could tell the Destroyer had managed to take out about five of the boats.

He organised his men and began firing onto the oncoming armada. The tanker was travelling at about fifteen knots and the attackers were buzzing around at nearly four times that speed, therefore, the chances of them actually hitting anything were pretty remote.

Four boats separated from the pack and opening the throttle, the loan driver of each headed for the hull of the tanker. The dinghies continued to accelerate, not varying from their course. The suicide bombers impacted with the hull almost simultaneously. The explosives went off within split seconds of each other. The men and boats exploded on impact. The hull was weakened and damaged and four ISIS members were dead.

"Here they come again," shouted the Captain.

Four more dinghies lined up with their suicidal skippers and accelerated towards the hull. The Jihadist were unflinching and unwavering. They aimed their vessels at precisely the same spot as the first wave. Again, four explosions ripped through the tanker. This time the outer skin was breached.

Eight suicidal bombers had died so far, but it was not to stop there. The third wave attacked and ripped into the hull enlarging the gaping wounds on the tanker. Twelve dead, sergeant Bootle wondered if they would continue in the same vain until they all died in a vain attempt to sink her.

The other dinghies kept up RGB and small arms fire, raining bullets and shrapnel onto the deck. One of the defenders took a bullet, but it was merely a flesh wound and a crew member got hit by flying glass. All in all the attack was seemingly ineffective. The Lynx helicopter launched by HMS Defender was having little success firing on the swarm of boats.

hen four more boats headed for the tanker. There was a difference, not one but two were on board. They weaved their way in and did not aim to crash into the hull but matched the speed of the tanker. The passenger seemed to be wearing a suicide vest. As each of the four dinghies manoeuvred alongside, the suicide bomber climbed into hole created by the previous bombings in the hull. It was not an easy, task two managed to board on the first attempt. The third fell into water once, was picked up and boarded on the second attempt. The last one took two swims before he finally boarded.

"I don't understand. Can they get on board?" Bootle asked.

"They are between the twin skins of the hull. Even if they blow a hole through they are above the water line," said the Captain.

"But the oil?"

"We are not carrying any. We just took on board seawater ballast to make it look like we were loaded. The owners did not want to risk the pollution."

"So what does happen if they blow a hole into the storage tanks?"

"Nothing, we will have a few holes to repair and I pump out the sea water. As the water is dispelled the tanker will rise higher above the water line as the ballast decreases. It was how the tanks were cleaned when the industry was less environmentally sound. Washing the oil out with seawater," said the captain. Four blasts interrupted them as the bombers blew themselves up. The small dinghies raced to shore having accomplished their mission.

They watched as the boats disappeared. Then the SS Rust Bucket exploded as a shell from the defender blew it out of the water. The captain and crew were long gone and the ship abandoned.

"Well we haven't sunk," said Bootle, "one in the eye for ISIS."

The radiation from the four dirty bombs was spreading throughout the tanker. The crew would soon start to feel the first signs of radiation sickness. The contamination would turn out to be so great that the tanker would eventually be declared a Total Loss. Two months later it would be towed out to the deep ocean where the sea cocks would be opened and would sink to its final resting place. The sea would dilute the effects of the radiation as it rusted into oblivion.

Chapter 38

"Come on," Jeff popped his head round the corner of Tim's office," Elaine wants us."

Tim secured the contents of his desk and put his Jacket on. They made their way to the lift. He was beginning to learn his way around the building and had only become lost twice that week. They knocked on her door and were called in.

"Morning boys," she was in cheery mood. She moved from behind her desk and they sat round the coffee table. Tim noticed that she was wearing a new pair of shoes. This he had learnt from past experience meant she was in a good mood. In fact, most of the staff had picked up on the mood shoe correlation. The arrival of new footwear would be spread around the office and people would greet their arrival by seeing her with anything that had gone wrong. Of course, you had to be quick as by lunchtime the shoe effect would be on the wane.

They sat and she volunteered to pour the coffee. She was definitely in a good mood. "Did you see the reports on the attack in the Gulf?"

"We did," said Jeff.

"It is odd to think that we are celebrating the failure of the Navy to protect an oil tanker though," said Tim.

"I know ,but it has all turned out so well. I have just heard from our insurance friends, they are very happy. Even though the tanker has not sunk as it is effectively been rendered unusable due its radioactive state, they have deemed it a Total Loss. The dodgy middle east insurers put in their claim and were immediately hit with twice the amount in counter claims" she said

"And?" prompted Stiles

"And, four insurers could not pay and are out of the market for good. Three, backed by their Government's Sovereign Wealth funds, have had to stump up an extra two billion dollars to meet the liabilities."

"So what was the bottom line?"

"The UK insurance market as a whole ended up nearly a billion and a half up in extra profit, the owners of the boat got there insurance paid in full and ISIS and their backers lost a few billion dollars."

"Everybody wins," said Tim.

"The Navy looked a bit rubbish though," said Stiles

"Well they are working on sorting the overheating problem out, but it could take a year or two."

"Well we can all sleep safely knowing if we are attacked by arctic penguins our ships will be able to repel them," Stiles joked.

Back at his desk Tim felt a sense of nervousness as he contemplated his intentions. He sat for a long while analysing his emotions. He knew what he wanted to do but was it morally right? In the final analysis he knew he was after payback and he knew that it was a base emotion, but there had to be a price to pay for your actions.

He picked up the phone and waited while it rang. "Jason, Tim," was the acknowledgement, followed by silence. Tim had to remind himself that as far as Jason was concerned he could not be aware of the extent of his betrayal to Mehmet and the Turks. He certainly did not know that Tim had the video of the murder of that innocent child.

Tim controlled his emotions and contrived to sound friendly. "I know that matters between us are a little tense, but I have been asked by my bosses to normalise the situation between us, so to speak."

"What do you suggest?" was the terse reply. Jason had hoped to avoid this conversation, but he realised that having an enemy in MI5 would permanently scupper any chance of getting back on the diplomatic gravy train.

"How about I pop over after work and we go out for a bite to eat and go through matters. Clear the air so to speak?"

There was a pause. "I am at the London flat tomorrow night, about eight?"

Tim put the phone down.

The rush hour had abated by quarter past seven the next evening when Tim emerged from the underground at the Barbican. The Barbican was a complex of flats, restaurants, music and a performing arts venue in the City of London. He made his way into the complex and walked in the direction of London Wall, which was where Jason's flat was located.

The complex had been built in the heart of the City, essentially as Council Housing. Very up market Council homes let from the start to Companies and the wealthy. When the right to buy policy was introduced, they had been snapped up by the wealthy tenants at bargain prices and today they were worth millions.

Tim put his hand in his jacket pocket and felt the cold butt of the Makarov. He felt nervous and excited. In his trouser pocket he had the USB card with the video of Jason's guilt tucked in the fold of his trouser pocket. He felt his legs slightly shaky beneath as his passed the restaurant and Arts centre and headed to the Tower block's entrance.

It was a little early so he paused to look at the water feature. He watched the fish swimming and the ducks, which had made this inner city sanctuary their home, paddle on the surface. A very tranquil scene, calming with glistening flecks of gold being reflected on the water's surface from the setting Sun. He was questioning himself. Could he really go through with this? He knew if he went further he would be changed for ever. Taken to a part of him, that once entered, could never be un-entered. He would cross a line that very few men do.

It was all so peaceful here. He looked at his watch, time to go. He walked to the entrance, selected the appropriate bell and pressed it. He waited.

"Hello," said Jason's voice over the intercom.

"It's Tim."

"OK, I'll buzz you in."

He took the lift and stepped out into a narrow corridor. He determined the way, the identical doors were numbered and taking a deep breath, went in the direction of Jason's flat. He pressed the buzzer and waited. He heard movement from behind the door and the sound of the lock being turned, the door started to open.

He became aware of a sudden movement from the periphery of his vision, then pain and black.

Chapter 39

He awoke feeling his way to consciousness. First confusion, vision blurred, mouth dry, pain in the head, a dull ache and then a feeling of nausea. Blind panic, as he found he was unable to move. He tried to lift his arms then his legs, something resisted his attempts to free his limbs. He couldn't understand. Where was he? Then Tim's memory returned.

The room came into view. It was large with a galley kitchen at one end and a French window at the other. Two ducks were settling down for the night on the balcony beyond the window. Behind them he could make out the skyline of the City. The room was expensively furnished in a minimalist style, themed black and white. The floor had been tiled in, obviously, very expensive Italian marble and the uncomfortable chairs were clearly of designer origin as was the glass and gold metal table.

He realised he was inside Jason's flat and tied to a chair. Further, on his left he realised Jason, completely naked, was also tied to a chair. He looked down. He at least had his clothes on. Although given his present predicament he was not altogether sure if that gave him any advantage. On the sofa facing him sat a lithe, powerful looking individual of obvious Arab descent. It was not a kind face looking at him, but Tim noticed that it was a handsome face with large oval eyes. The man was holding Tim's gun and his wallet.

"Welcome back Mr Burr," Annubis spoke. "Thank you for the gun by the way," he waved it from side to side.

Tim noticed that Jason's chest rose and fell as he breathed. At first he had thought him dead, but realised that he had also been knocked out. "Who are you?"

Annubis ignored the question and continued to look at Tim's wallet. "Mr MI5, what are you doing here?"

"I came to see Jason,"

"So you are friends?"

"Hardly," said Tim.

"Mr MI5, I think you should know what you tell me and say in the next few moments will determine if you live or die. I will not waste a great deal of my time asking you questions. When Mr Delonge awakens I shall be fully occupied, so you have a few moments only to convince me to let you live. Whilst I am a killer, I am not a homicidal maniac, I only kill for a reason. Please be frank and honest. I ask you one more time, are you friends with this man?"

Tim thought through his options and concluded there were none. He concluded that his only hope lay with the truth. Now in normal circumstances you do not admit to planning to murder someone, but given the fact that his captor seemed to have the same fate in mind as he did for Jason, he decided to be frank and honest.

"I am not friends with him. I hate this man. I came to kill him," he admitted to Annubis and to himself. He had not really considered what he had come to do was cold bloodied murder until this point. Hearing himself say it out loud changed something in him. He realised that he was capable of murder and that he was a different sort of person than he had lived his life believing he was.

"Why do you want to do that? Was it an order from MI5?"

"No, it is personnel," Jason groaned and Annubis looked over at the naked figure in the chair. "I suggest you tell me everything quickly, time is running out for our conversation."

"He was responsible for the death of a friend of mine called Yosuf and he betrayed us both to Turkish Intelligence."

"How did your friend die," the mention of the Turkish Secret Intelligence Service had intrigued Annubis. After all, it had been less than seventy two hours since he had killed their highest ranking field officer, Mehmet.

"Shot by a man called Mehmet Yildirim and his thugs on the streets of North London."

"You say this bit of shit in the chair over there is responsible?" Annubis waved the gun towards Jason.

"He betrayed me, left my out in the cold at the mercy of this Mehmet. Yosuf got me to England safely. He did not need to. He could have run and saved his own skin."

"You have a lot of hate Mr Burr for this man," reading his name from the ID he held. "But I cannot let you kill him before I ask him some questions. Depending on his answers, I may have to kill him my way."

"There is something more you should know about this man."

"I know a lot more than you think. For example I knew your late friend Mehmet."

"Late?"

"Oh yes, he came to terrible death a few days. Tortured, mutilated and killed"

"By you?"

"Yes I killed him," Annubis had no worry of admitting murder to Tim, because he could easily kill him and silence him forever. "He abused me has a child. He was a paedophile."

"I know," said Tim.

Annubis was surprised. "What else do you know?"

Tim realised from his admission that he had a chance of surviving as the man in front of him was on a revenge mission. Looking into those sad oval eyes, a suspicion began to form in his mind. "I know that Jason was also a molester of small boys and murdered one. That was the control Mehmet had over him."

Annubis's hands began to shake. This man in front of him was, more or less, confirming that Jason had murdered his young brother. He hardly dare ask "How do you know this for sure?"

"I have a video of the murder."

"Annubis was becoming almost uncontrollable with emotion. "Where is this video?" his voice was shaking.

Tim thought, he now knew for certain that this man in front of him was a relative of that small boy, brother, or a cousin. The more he looked at him, the more he could see the familiar resemblance. Knowing this, he had to somehow get himself out of this alive.

"I came here to kill this man for my friend and for the dreadful things he had done to an innocent child. It was not my plan to die doing it. I do not wish to die, but I am sure you will not hesitate to kill me."

Annubis put the gun down beside him and put his hand in his pocket, he pulled out a single feather. "I will not kill you," he said simply and blew the feather up towards the ceiling, "Lighter than a feather."

Tim looked at him baffled. It was clear though that this man was not completely sane. "Untie me and I will give you the video. "

"You will get the video and bring it to me? If I let you go, you will flee and go to the police."

"I may do the former, but I would be pretty stupid to do the latter," said Tim. "What should I say, 'Dear Mr Policeman, I was just about to murder a high ranking diplomat when I bumped into someone else who got there first.' That would not be the greatest idea in the World, would it?"

"That would be pretty stupid," Annubis agreed. He sat quietly and thought. He decided. He crossed the room to the kitchen area. Carrying a large knife he returned to Tim and cut his hands free. Tim rubbed his wrists and waited for the blood supply to return. He bent down and started to untie his ankles. Annubis retreated to the sofa and pointed the Makarov at him.

"You will retrieve the video and post it to me if I give you an address?" he asked

"That will not be necessary," said Tim, "I have it here."

Tim reached into his pocket and retrieved the USB memory stick. Annubis looked surprised. He had searched him thoroughly. The old magician's trick had worked again thought Tim, seeing the puzzled face before him.

Tim handed Annubis the stick and he handed Tim his wallet. "I shall keep the gun," Annubis said.

Annubis's hand was trembling as he put the stick into Jason's laptop that was sat on the overly ornate dining table. Tim turned away as the video loaded. He did not have the stomach to watch it a second time. Annubis let out a sort of anguished wailing noise as the small boy's image came onto the screen. He then sat unmoving as the horror unfolded before him. The tears slowly ran down his cheeks.

They sat in silence for a long while. Tim was unsure what to do next, waiting to see how this grief stricken man in front of him would react. Annubis was struggling to control his rage, his blood lust.

He spoke, "You need to go. I shall be here a while and you need to have an alibi. The City of London is covered by more CCTV than anywhere on the Planet. You will have been captured on video coming here. You must be seen leaving before he dies and you should make sure you have witnesses to your being elsewhere when he dies. Say, if asked, that you came to visit and when you left he was alive and well. Do you understand?"

Tim nodded and picking up his wallet, left. The last thing he saw was Annubis staring at Jason with hate in his eyes.

Chapter 40

The humidity earlier in the day had dissipated as Tim stepped from the Tower block. He looked at his watch, it was just before one in the morning. He made his way past the lake. The ducks were no longer present, but to the side he saw two glowing eyes. It was a fox on its nightly rounds, scavenging for food. He decided to retrace his route and headed across the complex. He would need a taxi at this time of night. He was aware now of the many CCTV cameras capturing him as he walked.

He reached the Barbican, but there was no sign of life. The City dies at night and all activity moves to the clubs, bars and theatres in the West End. He continued walking in his quest to find a taxi. He knew that his progress was being monitored on the cameras, providing him with the alibi he needed. A living witness would be helpful as well.

As he walked towards Clerkenwell, he began to hear the sound of voices. He followed his ears and the night club entrance came into view. A throng of people were waiting in the hope of gaining admission.

Three drunken young men were squaring off to the bouncers controlling the door. The three bouncers looked less than concerned and were just facing down the youths, who were swearing and issuing threats which they could not deliver. Tim saw the taxi rank just along the road past the club. There was a small queue and a couple of taxis. He made his way in that direction. A further argument was taking place between a cabbie and a couple of drunks, whom he had no wish to carry for fear of them vomiting in his taxi.

Tim became aware of the sound of a scuffle to his right as he walked to the rank. He looked down the street and saw, what appeared at first, a group of three people involved in a wrestling match. He then heard a woman's voice and then a male's.

"Stop it, bitch," shouted the male and then the sound of a slap.

The scene became clear. Two youths were holding a woman, pulling her dress open and struggling to pull her panties down. She only seemed partly aware what was happening to her. She seemed either high on drink or drugs. She was ineffectively trying to keep hold of her panties and dress while almost collapsing

The night was turning out to be more than he had bargained for, but he knew he had to get involved. It was clear this young woman was not a willing participant and he had no intention to walk on and let a rape occur. He ran towards the group.

"Stop that," he shouted.

"Fuck off, cunt," came the reply.

One of the youths, slightly taller than Tim, left his mate to carry on molesting the girl and ran to meet Tim.

It was clear to Tim that there was not to be a rational discussion on the matter, when he saw that his would be assailant was holding a beer bottle by the neck. His intention was to bash Tim's brains in with it. At last, thought Tim, an actual attack with a bottle. His chance to actually put into practice all those years of training in the dojo. He had fought in competitions and sparred, but never had he been in a street fight. He dropped into his stance without thinking. The moves were ingrained and required no thought. Hours of performing the Katas, the set routines designed to perfect movement of defence and attack, were about to be tested in the real world.

It was over in an instant. His assailant made no attempt to defend himself. Blinded by drunken rage he merely raced shouting obscenities at Tim. Seeing a man twenty years older, he assumed that he could easily intimidate him. He ran straight into Tim's kick to his chest. He looked surprised as the wind left his body and he collapsed gasping.

Tim was also surprised that his opponent fell so easily. In his sparring and competitions, he was used to his opponents being far more skilled at avoiding running into a simple kick. Tim was not in the best of moods and it released a bit of the tension he had experienced earlier, from being tied up by a homicidal maniac. He gave the yob a second kick in the stomach, ensuring that he wouldn't be indulging in any more bottle waving.

He jogged down to the other youth who was still molesting the woman. He realised Tim was there too late as his fist stuck him in the face, shattering his nose. Not strictly text book marshal art thought Tim but very satisfying. "Fuck off," said Tim. The yob looked at his mate rolling around on the ground and fucked off.

The young woman was in her early thirties and very pretty, with nice eyes, dark brown hair and a pretty mouth. She was tall, about five nine or ten Tim guessed. Very attractive he thought as he put his arm round her and pulled her dress over her exposed breast. He couldn't help noticing she had lovely breasts as well.

She seemed completely out of it. He could not smell any alcohol on her breath and she looked far too well dressed to be drug addict. He half carried her to the taxi rank and half dragged her to the front of the line.

He pushed aside the drunks still trying to force the cabbie to take them. There were disgruntled shouts from the rest of the line as he opened the door and got into the taxi with the woman. The taxi driver was about to say something about waiting in line, but decided he had enough of the altercations and he would be better off taking the fare he had on board.

"Where to?" he said.

Tim did not know where to. "Just head West while I get the address."

He opened the bag she had clung to throughout all the recent events and located her driving license. He gave the driver the address and studied it. She was thirty four and was called Jacqueline. He also found a picture of a small boy, about the same age as the boy in the video. This boy did not have the sad eyes and look of fear though. He put the photo back.

She was beginning to talk. It was clear that she was not a drinker or a drug user. He thought her drink may have been spiked, a growing problem in the pubs, bars and clubs in London these days.

She lived in Muswell Hill and the taxi took the route through Crouch End and up the hill to the Broadway. Tim did not know the area well, but seeing Alexander Palace, he had a good idea where he was. Her house turned out to be a small semi-detached and was modern in contrast to the older houses in the road. The two semis had been built on a site where one older house had formerly stood.

He helped her up the path, opened the door and aided her inside. The house was small, the front door opened onto a glass lobby with a toilet off, through the glass door into an L shaped living room with stairs on the right up to the bedrooms and bathroom. There was a separate kitchen off the dining area. The house was empty. He would later learn she was divorced with a nine year old son, who at that moment was staying at his grandparents.

He helped her to her bedroom and taking her shoes off, left her to sleep. He left his phone number and a short note saying he would not mind meeting up for a drink. He waited outside for Uber to deliver his ride home. "Who knows what might come of it. It would be nice just to be normal for a bit," he thought.

Chapter 41

Annubis sat unmoving, watching Jason as he struggled to consciousness. He thought of his brother, so young, so vulnerable, so innocent. He thought of his Mother and his Father, of their home that was taken from them, along with their lives. He thought of his Country, that was now a perpetual war zone, fought over by bands of murderous bigots. He thought of all the death he had seen and all the death he had been responsible for.

Time passed and Jason struggled, unable to cry out with the pillow case stuffed in his mouth as a gag. He was in pain, cramp had set in, the blood flow was cut off from his hands and feet with the tightness of his bonds. Annubis watched as he thrashed around. Watching him first piss himself then defecate in fear. He was unmoved.

Hours passed. Still he waited.

The sun shone through the French window leading to the balcony. The ducks woke early and with a flap of their wings, flew down to the water feature and lake below. A new day dawns and the time ends for Annubis. The years of hate, the years of searching were at an end. He still could not act.

Hate had sustained him for so long, given him purpose and a reason to be. Now, he feared its passing. How would he live? Did he want to live? He had never thought beyond this point.

He decided to finish it. It roused himself and undressed, he knew

197

he could not leave here and walk through the City covered in blood. Naked it would be easy to shower, redress and leave.

He picked up the knife and moved towards Jason. He watched, savouring the fear in his eyes. He had planned a slow and agonising death, but his rage exploded like a torrent flowing along a jagged river bed. It would stop for nothing, scouring the rocks, destroying any obstacle that sought to slow its course. He stabbed and hacked and carried on cutting the body after Jason was long dead. The sweat poured from him as he carried on his rampage.

He stopped, the anger gone. Quiet now, only the beating of his heart filled the silence. He looked at the mutilated body and felt sick at his own actions, but cleansed in the blood that covered him. The room was red, walls, ceiling and the Italian marble floor.

He stood in the shower and allowed the warm water to wash it all away. He sank into the foetal position and began to cry. It seemed he would never stop. The water, the tears and the blood mixed and washed away. It washed it all away. He was Mem again.

He dressed and with sadness placed the white feather on the corpse.

Chapter 42

Wood Street Police Station was conveniently located for the Barbican just off London Wall and opposite the complex. Tim had a phone call earlier in the day, asking if he would provide a statement regarding the death of Jason Delonge. Normally the police would have just turned up and asked him questions. However, given that he worked in Thames House, MI5's headquarters, just turning up and wandering in off the street, even if you are policemen is not quite that simple. Tim had therefore agreed to attend the police station. That again had turned out to be less than simple. Because Tim worked for the Secret Intelligence Service, there was a protocol to follow. He was to be accompanied by a solicitor who specialised in the law and practice surrounding the Official Secrets Act and a senior MI5 employee to advise him on any aspect of National Security.

Tim, Stiles as the Deputy Head of MI5 and the solicitor sat together on one side of the interview table. A Detective Inspector and his sergeant sat on the other.

"We should like to record the interview," said the DS.

The solicitor intervened. "It is probably best that you don't. Should Mr Burr inadvertently say something in his reply that has security implications, it will be more difficult for us all to rectify the matter? In any event, I understand that Mr Burr is being interviewed as a witness only?"

The tape and video feed were turned off.

"What was your relationship with Mr Delonge?" asked the DI.

"Former colleagues at the Paris Embassy, I worked there for two and a bit years while Jason was Ambassador"

"What was the nature of your work?"

"Can't really let him answer that," said the solicitor.

"I meant, were you in regular contact with the deceased? Did you know him well?"

"Virtually every day and we were well acquainted."

"Friends?"

"I would not say that, more associates, brought into each other's company through our work."

"Did you regularly meet up socially?"

"No, not really, it was mostly work related as I said."

"And yet we have you on CCTV visiting Mr Delonge on the night of his murder. Why the sudden desire to call round?"

Tim realised when the Police had called earlier that his visit to Jason would clearly flag up as unusual behaviour and had expected to be questioned in detail about it, especially as he would have been the last person to see him alive, apart from his killer. "I had not seen him since Monte Carlo where we had been on a Trade Mission. My departure was sudden and subsequently, I was transferred to Thames House. In essence I hadn't said goodbye. He had returned to London, I gave him a ring and he invited me round for a drink and a catch up chat."

"You say your departure was sudden. Was there some sort of falling out or argument between you?" asked the DI.

"That one I cannot allow to be answered. I can say that Mr Burr was acting under instructions from MI5 and was recalled to London," said Stiles.

Tim was glad for the intervention. He could hardly have answered that Jason had set him up for the chop by the Turkish Secret Service and ISIS and still sounded like they were friends.

"Turning to the night of the murder, would you tell us exactly what occurred?"

"I got to Jason's and he invited me in for a drink."

"Do you remember what it was exactly you had to drink?"

Tim realised that he had created a problem for himself. He had no idea what drinks Jason had in his flat. If he said he had a whisky and there was no whisky he would be caught in a lie. He had no choice but to guess a beverage, "white wine."

"Did Mr Delonge have a drink as well?"

"Yes."

The DI looked down at the file in front of him. "And yet there were no used glasses found at the scene?"

"He must have washed up after I left."

"Possibly, there were no wine glasses in the dish washer. It was loaded with other dirty dishes that the cleaner takes care of when she comes in daily to tidy the flat," said the DS.

"What did you talk about?"

Stiles coughed and the DI changed the question. "Was Mr Delonge concerned about anything? Was he agitated in anyway?"

"It was a perfectly normal conversation. We laughed and joked about some of the goings on when we were in Paris. You know just a drink and a chat."

"Was there nothing at all odd in his behaviour?"

"Nothing"

"Did he say if he was expecting anyone?"

"No, when I left I had the impression that he was going to go to bed."

"So he was fit and well when you left?"

"Definitely," he lied. Well as fit and well as anyone could be, tied up and naked with a knife wielding homicidal maniac keeping you company, he thought.

"Where did you go after leaving?"

Tim gave his account of the incident outside the night club and taking the young woman home in the cab. The Police had recovered the CCTV footage from the club and the surrounding area and had already traced his movements.

"Thank you for your time," said the DI

They took their farewells and they headed back to Thames House by taxi.

"He is lying about something" said the DS

"Obviously, but there is nothing we can do. The video evidence clearly places him nowhere near the murder scene. The autopsy shows that Delonge died hours after he left. "But he knows something, but there is no way for us to be able to pursue it further."

Chapter 43

"Hello"

"Is that Anthony Burr?"

He replied that it was but was slightly suspicious as he did not recognise the voice, which usually meant a call centre and a tedious conversation about a prize he had won in a competition he had neither heard of nor entered.

"This is Jackie, the person you rescued and took home? I found your note and rang to thank you."

He had been pleased to hear from her and the conversation had gone well. He was sat in a small French Bistro style restaurant in Hampstead. He made an effort and looking in the mirror before he left, he decided he was passable. It was a warm evening and he had decided on the casual summer look. Light trousers, brown loafers, a light blue shirt with a jumper. He had not been on a date in over a year and felt a slight lack of confidence that comes from being ignored by the opposite sex for a long period.

He saw her enter and recognised her immediately. She was very pretty, far more attractive than he remembered. He had to admit though, the last time he had seen her she had not been at her best. He also had to admit he had been in an unusual frame of mind having just left Jason's flat.

He waved to her and seeing him, she crossed the dining room to his table. He stood up and greeted her with the customary three kiss, kiss, and kiss on the cheek greeting. Her hair was nicely cut and framed a beautiful face with large eyes and full lips. She wore a soft white shirt and a light warmer skirt that fell just below the knees. Attractive but classy he thought.

"Hi," she said. She looked at him and smiled.

It was a nice smile and Tim knew he really liked the look of this woman. "Can I order you a drink?"

"Just water," she answered. Tim, who had driven to the restaurant, was also on water. The waiter approached and handed them the menu and took the drinks order

"I do not usually drink," she continued.

"But when you do?" he left the sentence hanging.

She smiled slightly embarrassed. "I had not been drinking when you found me outside the club. I really don't know what happened. I had gone out after work with some colleagues to celebrate getting a new audit client"

"You're an accountant?"

"I know, not very exciting is it? I've just been made a junior partner in a small City firm. What do you do?"

"A civil servant, even less exciting, I am afraid. Please continue."

"I had one glass of Champagne in the local by the office and some food. At closing, a few decided to go onto the club. Now I haven't been to a nightclub in years. Why not I said to myself? My son Daniel was staying round my parents, so for once, I did not need to be home."

"Your son, how old is he?"

"He is nine? Before you ask his Dad is not about and hasn't been about for years."

Tim realised that she was observant. She was right, he was angling to know if she was unattached and she had answered his question. He put out his situation to let her know that he was on the market. "I am divorced and my wife has remarried."

She looked at him and smiled. He was encouraged. "Where was I? Oh yes, my wild night out. I remember going to the club and thinking I am too old for this and deciding I would call it a night, when a chap came over and offered me a drink. I thought what the hell, he was quite good looking."

She paused, "That sounded bad, I am not in the habit of picking up random strangers."

"Apart from me?" said Tim.

"You're right; I am in the habit of picking up random strangers it seems. Anyway, I took the drink. Then zilch, nothing, I don't remember a thing. I don't remember leaving. I have no idea how I got outside with the two chaps. It is a total blank."

"It was probably a spiked drink? All too common these days, but all's well that ends well. The bonus is that I got to meet a very beautiful woman." Jackie looked at him and moved her hand to her hair and twilled it between her fingers. He really did find her very attractive.

He had driven her back from the restaurant and she had invited him in for coffee. She had started to show him the house then realised that he was already familiar with it. Slightly embarrassed by the memory that the last time he was here was when he had to haul her incoherently up the stairs and get her to bed. She retreated to the kitchen to make the coffee.

There was an awkward period when the conversation flagged. They both knew that they wished to get a little closer, but how to get from a cup of coffee to embracing was proving to be cumbersome.

Tim decided to just go for the honest approach. "I really want to kiss you," he said.

"I want you to."

They kissed and then kissed some more. He was becoming very aroused and she could feel his erection pressing into her as they pulled each other close. She wanted this man. It had been a very long time since she had felt such an intense desire. Her husband had left her battered bruised and bereft of any self-confidence. Now, suddenly, she felt like a woman again and a desirable woman at that.

She took his hand and took him to the bedroom. She wanted him and she felt free to want him. She felt liberated from the controlling restraint of her husband who was derisive and gradually made her feel worthless. The look in Tim's eyes, his obvious admiration and desire for her was a healing force.

She sat him before her on her bed and with a brazenness she had never exhibited before in her life, began to strip for him. She did it deliberately, taking pleasure in playing the exhibitionist, slowly unbuttoning her blouse and dropping it to the floor. Then she turned her back to him, she allowed her skirt to fall, gyrating her bottom to aid its descent. She undid the clasp on her bra, her nipples so erect it clung to them before falling.

Again she turned her back and bending she removed her knickers, lingering to allow her bottom to be fully exposed as she bent down, legs straight to free the panties from her shoes. His heart was pounding as she turned and bent forward kissing him.

She undid his shirt buttons and pulled his shirt off and began to rub her breasts against his bare chest. His trousers, shoes and socks were difficult to undo, he decided he could not take too much more and rapidly undressed himself. Her naked body against his felt so right, so good and so sensual as he pushed her down into the softness of the bed.

He woke the next morning before she did and he watched the rise and fall of her breathing, the curve of her bottom and waist. Her hair messed up on the pillow. He really did like this woman. He curled himself round her body and feeling secure and whole, fell back to sleep.

Printed in Great Britain
by Amazon